Carlto

"Easily the craziest, weirdest, strangest, funniest, most obscene writer in America."
—*GOTHIC MAGAZINE*

"Carlton Mellick III has the craziest book titles... and the kinkiest fans!"
—CHRISTOPHER MOORE, author of *The Stupidest Angel*

"If you haven't read Mellick you're not nearly perverse enough for the twenty first century."
—JACK KETCHUM, author of *The Girl Next Door*

"Carlton Mellick III is one of bizarro fiction's most talented practitioners, a virtuoso of the surreal, science fictional tale."
—CORY DOCTOROW, author of *Little Brother*

"Bizarre, twisted, and emotionally raw—Carlton Mellick's fiction is the literary equivalent of putting your brain in a blender."
—BRIAN KEENE, author of *The Rising*

"Carlton Mellick III exemplifies the intelligence and wit that lurks between its lurid covers. In a genre where crude titles are an art in themselves, Mellick is a true artist."
—*THE GUARDIAN*

"Just as Pop had Andy Warhol and Dada Tristan Tzara, the bizarro movement has its very own P. T. Barnum-type practitioner. He's the mutton-chopped author of such books as *Electric Jesus Corpse* and *The Menstruating Mall*, the illustrator, editor, and instructor of all things bizarro, and his name is Carlton Mellick III."
—*DETAILS MAGAZINE*

Also by Carlton Mellick III

Satan Burger
Electric Jesus Corpse
Sunset With a Beard (stories)
Razor Wire Pubic Hair
Teeth and Tongue Landscape
The Steel Breakfast Era
The Baby Jesus Butt Plug
Fishy-fleshed
The Menstruating Mall
Ocean of Lard (with Kevin L. Donihe)
Punk Land
Sex and Death in Television Town
Sea of the Patchwork Cats
The Haunted Vagina
Cancer-cute (Avant Punk Army Exclusive)
War Slut
Sausagey Santa
Ugly Heaven
Adolf in Wonderland
Ultra Fuckers
Cybernetrix
The Egg Man
Apeshit
The Faggiest Vampire
The Cannibals of Candyland
Warrior Wolf Women of the Wasteland
The Kobold Wizard's Dildo of Enlightenment +2
Zombies and Shit
Crab Town
The Morbidly Obese Ninja
Barbarian Beast Bitches of the Badlands
Fantastic Orgy (stories)
I Knocked Up Satan's Daughter
Armadillo Fists
The Handsome Squirm
Tumor Fruit
Kill Ball
Cuddly Holocaust
Hammer Wives (stories)
Village of the Mermaids
Quicksand House
Clusterfuck
Hungry Bug

THE TICK PEOPLE

CARLTON MELLICK III

ERASERHEAD PRESS
PORTLAND, OREGON

ERASERHEAD PRESS
205 NE BRYANT
PORTLAND, OR 97211

WWW.ERASERHEADPRESS.COM

ISBN: 978-1-62105-145-9

AUTHOR'S NOTE

I wrote *The Tick People* earlier this month when I needed to step away from a larger project to write something shorter. It seems all of my books keep getting longer and longer these days, so it's good to focus on something of novella size for a week or so in order to get a boost of confidence from completing something new. If I'm not finishing projects on a regular basis, I tend to go a little nuts. It probably stems from my deep irrational fear that I only have a few months left to live and need to accomplish as much as possible before I die.

Right now, I'm going between smoking e-cigarettes and real cigarettes—the e-cigarettes are for when I don't want to go outside—reflecting on why the hell I wrote yet another weird sex book. If you didn't notice, my last six or seven books didn't include much (or any) sex at all, so maybe it was past due. I knew I wanted to write about a man's struggle against his own sexual urges. I wondered what it would be like if a man's carnal desires were warped. What if, instead of being sexually drawn to women, there was a guy who was drawn to something repulsive and inhuman, something his mind knows is utterly disgusting but his body can't resist. I wanted to explore the absurdity of sexual desire. Sure we humans might seem like sexy nubile creatures most of the time, but when you think about it, we're really just sweaty blobs of gross. Why the hell do we bother having sex with each other? There's creating children, sure, but how many kids do we really need? Two or three? Couldn't we just divide like amoebas or something?

Perhaps this theme is important to me because I have recently discovered that I have a deep instinctual urge to mate with McDonald's McRib sandwiches. They're only two for three dollars right now. I think I'll have a threesome.

—Carlton Mellick III 3/11/2014 12:14am

CHAPTER ONE
THE SADDEST DOG IN GLOOM TOWN

There was once a dog named Old Gloomy who was so big, so mind-spinningly enormous, that he was mistaken for a mountain top. Nobody ever suspected the soft, fluffy mountain peak to actually be a living animal, despite the fact that its soil was abnormally warm and grew fields of fuzzy brown fur. If the people of Fluffville would have known the mountain was actually alive, they never would have built their city around the massive canine. And if Old Gloomy would have known he would be mistaken for a mountain top, he never would have taken such a deep long snooze.

It was quite a surprise to the citizens of Fluffville when the massive beast awoke after its century-long nap, sniffing at the delicious meaty aroma billowing out of the mutton stew factory that stood on the tip of its nose. It licked its school-covered lips and blinked away the suburban crust that had collected in its eyes.

The town was immediately evacuated in a quiet, tip-toeing panic. Everyone thought their beautiful city would be destroyed by the waking behemoth as they waited outside city limits. But days passed and nothing happened. The weight of the city's architecture was so heavy that it pinned Old Gloomy to his spot. And no matter how much his howls and whines rumbled the countryside, the dog could not break free. He was forever trapped beneath the great city and forced to spend the rest of his days as a living mountain top.

Life was not easy for the citizens of Fluffville once they went back to their old lives knowing full well their homes were built on top of the giant dog. They could hear the thunderous heartbeat pulsing through their walls at night. On the drive to work, they could feel the ground swelling up and down beneath their cars as the earth breathed. The air reeked of wet dog whenever it rained. Their livestock was blown out of the pastures whenever the dog coughed or sneezed.

But the worst part of living on Old Gloomy was the sadness that lingered in the air. The melancholy radiated out of the giant dog all day and all night, hovering over the city like a cloud of emotional pollution. This was how the town earned the nickname *Gloomville*—the gloomiest of all gloomy places to live in the world.

But it was very important to keep Old Gloomy as sad as possible. You see, whenever the dog was happy he wagged his tail with excitement. This caused a tornado of destruction, smashing apart the downtown shopping district and toppling high-rise apartment buildings. So in order to prevent this disaster from continuing, it became every citizen's duty to keep Old Gloomy's spirits as low as they could possibly go.

There was even a team of professional sadness-makers, paid by the city, who were tasked with keeping the dog in a state of constant depression. All day, they would call him a bad dog and scold him for things he didn't even do. They would feed him only the blandest, driest, most sorrow-filled kibble. Then they would show him videos of happy dogs, running and playing in the sunlight, reminding Old Gloomy of all the things he couldn't possibly do in his condition. A working day wasn't over until the old dog's eyes opened up into thick salty waterfalls.

Fernando Mendez was one of these sadness-makers—officially known as Stressmen. He took pride in his job, just as his father had when he was a Stressman, and his grandfather before him. He enjoyed the respect he received from his neighbors whenever he was out mowing his brown-fur lawn. He was treated like a hero whenever he went down to the pub for a dog-tear brew after a long day of work.

But something had changed in Fernando after his tenth

year on the job. He started feeling sorry for Old Gloomy. Instead of depressing the dog, he found himself yearning to cheer him up. He wanted to see a happy expression spread across his face just once. Sometimes, he lay awake at night dreaming about what would happen if he bought Old Gloomy a giant rubber ball to play with or gave him a great big doggy treat for him to munch on. But Fernando knew this could never be. He had to keep his community safe.

"Old Gloomy's suffering must never end." That's what was written above his locker when he arrived at work every day.

Fernando looked at himself in the mirror, placing the saddest frown he could muster onto his face. His uniform was a dark emotionless gray, with a despairing design somewhere between that of a mortician and an imperial officer posted on the Death Star.

A plump man with long fisherman whiskers appeared behind him in the mirror. "You're late, Mendez. The third time this week. What's gotten into you? You're supposed to be my top Stressman."

It was Mr. Olsen, the boss—an old bastard who'd been a Stressman for as long as anyone could remember. He worked with both Fernando's father and grandfather. When he came to work, he didn't have to put on a frown to start his day. He had a natural talent for being miserable.

"I've been feeling under the weather," Fernando said. It was clearly a lie, but he could never admit the truth to his boss. He couldn't tell him that his heart just wasn't in the job anymore.

Mr. Olsen didn't buy the excuse, but let the issue go. "So what did you come up with? It better be something good."

"This one will work."

"You said that last time."

"This will work better than last time."

One of the jobs of the Stressmen was to come up with new and creative methods for depressing Old Gloomy. They couldn't use the same techniques time after time. When overused, the dog would become numb to their sadness treatments and they would no longer be effective. So they had to continuously brainstorm new ideas each year in order to keep the mutt down in the dumps.

"The lives of thousands of people are at stake, Mendez. That dog better be crying by lunchtime or it's your ass."

Fernando deepened his frown and nodded softly. "This will work. I'll stake my career on it."

"You're damn right you will."

Then the miserable old man poured himself a cup of oily, flavorless coffee and stole the entire plate of cake doughnuts before Fernando could claim one.

Fernando stepped outside of Stressman Headquarters onto the platform below Old Gloomy's massive left eye. When the dog saw him, he let out a deep sigh that vibrated through the facility. The old boy knew what was coming next—something dismal was about to be forced upon him. The dog immediately closed his eyes so that he wouldn't have to watch, but they both knew his efforts were in vain.

"I'll take care of it, Mr. Mendez," said a voice from the control tower.

It was Johnson. Fernando's young assistant who started last year. The kid was bright, but not too good at his job. Like many young people, he was a bit too optimistic and enjoyed life too much to be an effective Stressman. He knew how to operate the equipment and assist Fernando with adequacy, but he needed his dreams crushed and his heart broken a few more times before he'd be capable of performing a professional-level sadness treatment on his own.

"Take your time, Jake," Fernando called up as he climbed the ladder to the control tower. "There's no hurry."

Fernando's father taught him that a good Stressman always worked at a lethargic pace, with no excitement, no energy. His job was not just to keep the animal sad, but to keep him bored and without stimulation.

"Yes, Mr. Mendez."

In the control tower, Jake Johnson pulled levers and tapped buttons, listening to mournful violin music as he operated the cranes that pulled open Gloomy's left eyelid. They wouldn't be able to show the dog sad things if the beast kept his eyes closed all day. Not only that, but they didn't want Gloomy falling asleep before he was sufficiently depressed. They couldn't allow an opportunity for good dreams.

"That'll do," Fernando said behind the assistant, once the eyelid was propped all the way open. "Now raise the screen."

As Johnson hit the switch to raise the movie screen, Fernando looked up into the colossal orb before him. The eye was like a murky brown lake, so big that Fernando could jump inside of it and swim across the ever-moist pupil. Whenever he looked at the giant dog eye-to-eye, Fernando always wondered what the dog thought of them. They were merely fleas to the massive beast; fleas that he could never scratch away.

"So what have you got today?" Johnson asked.

Fernando opened his briefcase and flipped through his data disks, each one containing a different sadness treatment.

"Put this one on first," he said, handing his assistant a disk.

When Johnson put in the disk, a movie was projected across the screen. It was a short film of a dog that resembled Old Gloomy. He was having a birthday party, sitting beside a cake with a party hat dangling off the side his head. But it was not a happy party. Nobody showed up to the dog's birthday because he doesn't have any friends. The doggy made the cake for himself and was celebrating his birthday by himself, lying by the cake with a lonely expression on his face, jowls drooping against the floor, too sad to even take a lick of the frosting.

"Is it working?" Johnson asked.

Fernando looked at the monitor and shook his head. "The readings show no change in mood."

"But the loneliness theme usually works," Johnson said.

"He's tuning it out. We need something sadder."

They tried another film. This one was about a puppy who gets separated from his mother. He spends days searching for his family, wandering through the desolate wasteland, being as lonely as a pup could be. But then it turns out that the whole area is highly radioactive and the dog gets really sick. His skin falls off and he drags his body across the desert like a living skeleton.

"Geez, Mr. Mendez," Johnson said as they watched the film. "This one's pretty dark."

When the puppy finally reaches his mother, the momma dog doesn't recognize the puppy and growls at it, threatening to rip his throat out. No matter how much the puppy begs and pleads with his momma, she refuses to believe it's her son. She abandons the pup in the barren landscape, leaving him to die a long, painful death. Alone.

Johnson was tearing up by the end of the film, but Old Gloomy's mood did not change. The dog just let out another long sigh.

"It didn't affect him," Johnson said, wiping his tears away.

Fernando said, "He's just getting bored."

"I thought bored was good?"

"Bored is okay, but we don't get paid until he cries."

"Do you have anything sadder?"

"Not really." Fernando looked through the disks and grabbed one at random. "Just put this one on."

The film they played featured a dog that discovers a mountain of food filled with giant bones, hot dogs, and slabs of meat. The dog happily runs around the food with his tongue dangling out, salivating all over the place. But as soon as the dog takes a bite of a hot dog, it turns to ash. The dog goes after a juicy steak, but it's the same result. Everything he tries to eat disintegrates in his mouth before he gets a chance to taste it.

"Something's happening," Johnson said, examining the monitor.

But Fernando didn't have to look at the readings to notice the change in Old Gloomy's mood. He could see it plain as day. The dog's massive eye quivered. His breathing became heavy.

"Is he about to cry?" Johnson yelled, turning around to the control panel that operated the aqueduct. "Should I open the flood gate?"

"No..." Fernando could tell something was wrong. The dog wasn't getting sad. He was getting hungry. "Quick, turn off the film!"

"What?"

"The food's making him excited!"

"But it's not real food. It turns into ash before the dog can eat it."

"Just turn it off!"

Fernando hit the switch himself, removing the film from the projector, but it was too late. The dog was panting heavily, excited by the images of all those bones and meats.

Mr. Olsen's voice came over the intercom system. "What the hell is going on up there, Mendez?"

Fernando ignored his boss. He went to the monitoring station, looking at the video feed from the tail-section of town. The ground was beginning to quake. The buildings in the shopping district shuddered and rumbled. He could see people running for their lives.

"His tail's about to wag," Fernando said, trying to keep calm.

"What do we do?" Johnson cried.

Although the movie with the food was turned off, Old Gloomy held onto the memory of its images. Fernando could see it all over the dog's face. He could tell it was imagining what it would be like to eat all of that delicious food. Old Gloomy drooled into the canal below its jowls, then licked its lips with its massive goopy tongue.

"Give him the shot," Fernando said.

"The shot? Are you kidding?"

"We don't have a choice."

Johnson opened the emergency panel and hit the red button. A syringe the size of a tanker truck was launched at the dog's throat like a missile. It pierced its thick hide and green fluids blasted into the beast's bloodstream. Within seconds, the dog was knocked unconscious. The tail went limp before it even rose off the ground.

"The sedative worked," Johnson said. "His heart rate is lowering."

Fernando nodded, but didn't say anything, removing his hat and rubbing his fingers through the sweat in his hair. He cursed himself for not thinking things through when he put together that last video. Of course the food images would excite Old Gloomy. He felt like such an idiot. His father would have beaten him senseless if he were alive to see his son make such a stupid mistake.

"Do you know how much it costs the city to make just one dose of that sedative?" Mr. Olsen scolded Fernando. They were in the privacy of his office, but the boss was yelling at him so loud that all Stressmen in the station could hear.

"I know…" Fernando said.

"No, I *don't* think you know." Olsen pointed his chubby finger in Fernando's face. "If you take all of our annual salaries and multiply them by ten, *that's* how much taxpayer money goes into producing a single shot. And this is the second dose we used this year. The mayor is going to want my head for this."

Fernando had nothing to say in his defense. "I know I screwed up. It was a stupid mistake."

"Stressmen can't afford to make mistakes," Olsen said. "If a doctor makes a mistake, he could lose a patient. If a cop makes a mistake, an innocent man might spend the rest of his life in jail. If a Stressman makes a mistake, thousands of people die, a district is wiped out, and the city's economy goes to hell."

"Nobody died," Fernando said. "There was no damage."

"This time there wasn't, but that was our last shot. It could be months until we get another. If that dog feels another burst of joy before then, there *will* be damages. There *will* be deaths. And it will be your fault."

Fernando locked eyes with his boss. The man's forehead bulged with pulsing angry veins. His skin was wrinkled but tough like cowhide.

Fernando broke eye contact. "It won't happen again."

"Of course it won't happen again. You're on suspension without pay until further notice."

"Are you serious?"

"Damn right I'm serious. The only reason I'm not firing you is out of respect for your father. You're lucky he's not alive to see what a fuckup you've become."

Fernando looked down at his hands and shut his mouth tight before he opened it and said something that he'd regret. He knew Mr. Olsen was just giving him a hard time so that he'd never make the same mistake again.

"I understand," Fernando said.

The boss turned away from him, going toward his filing cabinet to get back to work.

"Go home," Olsen told him in a softer tone. "Take some time off. Watch some depressing movies or something. Then I want you to think about what it really means to be a Stressman. I can't use you unless your head's in the game."

Fernando nodded. Then he left the room. The last thing he wanted to do was think about what it really meant to be a Stressman. That kind of thinking was what weakened his resolve in the first place.

CHAPTER TWO
BACKBONE

That night, Fernando went for a few beers at Backbone Tavern which was located in the center of Old Gloomy's spine. Thick, coarse hair grew from the ground like bamboo here, covering the hard mountainous ridges that jutted out of the earth like boulders of bone.

"Keep them coming," Fernando said to the bartender, as he guzzled down the dog-tear brews.

Everyone in the place was giving him dirty looks. They knew the earthquake that day was his fault. They could tell by the way he was drinking in his profoundly guilty manner. Normally the customers were very respectful and proud of their neighborhood Stressman, but whenever Old Gloomy did something wrong they'd all turn on him in an instant, quick to make him a target of abuse. Not even the bartender would talk to him when he ordered his drinks.

"What a disgrace…" He thought he heard somebody say. "Stressmen these days just aren't what they used to be."

He wasn't sure if that was something somebody was really saying or if his subconscious was altering their words. Either way, Fernando didn't look at them. He just kept drinking.

The beer served in many Gloomville taverns were brewed using Gloomy's tears instead of water. It gave the brew a thick, rich flavor, which most people found to be unpleasant. Personally, Fernando loved the flavor of the salty wheat beer as long as he didn't think too hard about how he was drinking fermented body fluids that leaked from a giant mammal. But whether the flavor was good or bad didn't matter. The point of brewing with Old Gloomy's tears was because it was believed to cause sadness in those who consumed them. Since happiness was not socially acceptable in Gloomville, bartenders had to be extra careful about what kind of liquor they served. They wanted their customers to become sad-drunk, not happy-drunk.

When Fernando's sister arrived at the bar, he'd already taken down several beers. However, he was not nearly as drunk as he wanted to be. She glared at him with her penetrating librarian eyes.

"How have you been, Little Bro?" Bethany asked in her precise, condescending manner. She wiped the snowball-sized dog dander from her business skirt and sat down beside him. "I see you've gotten started without me."

Bethany was not too happy to see so many empty beer glasses on her brother's table. She knew he'd just been suspended from work, but it wasn't like him to solve his problems with alcohol.

"How long have you been here?" she asked.

"Long enough to get cut off if I was in any other bar," he said.

She snapped her thin pointy fingers at the bartender and ordered a drink using her own version of sign language. Then she looked back at her brother. "When did you become so pathetic?"

He tossed the rest of his beer down his throat. "About two hours ago."

"Well, you're thirty years old. You should start acting like it."

"I'm not thirty yet."

"You will be at Midnight."

The bartender brought Bethany her drink and another for Fernando.

"Happy Birthday to me," he said, raising his eyebrows as he brought the fresh beer to his lips.

"You know why I wanted to meet you today, don't you?"

"I know it wasn't to give me a birthday present."

"You made a promise to me and I'm here to make sure you keep it."

"What promise was that?"

Bethany took the tiniest sip of her beverage and wrinkled her lips at the flavor.

"Don't play dumb with me," she said. "You know exactly what I'm talking about. You've promised me for years that once you turned thirty you would register with the Matchmaking Bureau."

Fernando sighed and dropped his head to the table. "This again…"

"Yes, this again."

He raised his head and took a long sip. He was too drunk and emotionally exhausted to be having this conversation. "I said I'd do it once I was in my thirties. Not on my thirtieth birthday."

"Well, once Midnight comes you'll be in your thirties."

He held up his hands. "Look, I'll think about it. That's the best you're going to get out of me right now. I don't have time to deal with the Matchmaking Bureau and all that bullshit."

"Actually, now that you're indefinitely suspended I believe it's a perfect time to register with the Matchmaking Bureau."

Fernando shook his head. "I'm not doing it. No way."

"Well, you don't have a choice. I've already set up an appointment for you."

He raised his voice. "Are you kidding me?"

The other patrons of the bar looked over at them, but he didn't care.

Bethany pulled the paperwork out of her briefcase. "The fee, as you know, wasn't cheap. Consider it your birthday present."

"That's the worst present you've ever given me."

"It's the only birthday present I've ever given you. But it's also the best you could ever receive. You'll thank me for it later."

"I can't believe you're doing this to me. Are you sure you can't push the date back? To next Fall maybe?"

"No, you have to go tomorrow. Otherwise, you owe me two thousand dollars for the fee. If you don't want to go that's fine, but I'll expect a check by the end of the week."

Fernando had to laugh. Even though it was not a happy laugh, the bartender gave him a dirty look for laughing in his cheer-free establishment.

"They'll fit you with a mold in the morning and if your matchmate is in the system, which I'm sure she'll be, then you'll know who you're destined to be with by the afternoon."

"I'm not ready to start a family."

"You don't have to start a family right away. If you don't like her you don't have to start a family at all. But it's important to get yourself in the system."

"Why? If I'm not interested in starting a family then what's the point?"

"You're not going to do it for you. You're going to do it for her. I know what it's like to wait for my matchmate. Somewhere out there is a poor girl who's been waiting her entire life for you. She can't marry anyone else. She can't have children with anyone else. She can only be with you. She probably registered when she was eighteen years old like most girls do. And ever since then she's been waiting to learn who she was meant to spend her life with. You've seen those depressed girls in the Matchmate Bureau commercials. That's how I was for years. It was like I was living in limbo until Harry finally registered."

Fernando had gotten lectured a thousand times before. Usually, he just ignored her. This time he tried to argue. "But she could have died as a child for all I know. Or she could live on the other side of the world. Or she could be in love with another man even if he's not her matchmate."

"Yeah, and if that's the case you'll be off the hook. But you need to register so you know for sure. You just can't leave that girl hanging any longer."

"But what if I don't like her?"

"I was worried about that too before I met Harry, but look at us now. We're perfect for each other."

"You said you didn't like him the first time you met him."

"Well, not when I first laid eyes on him. He was out of shape and had horrible fashion sense. But that was just superficial. By the end of our first date, I could feel the connection between us. I knew we were two parts of the same whole."

Fernando looked down at his drink. Bethany placed her hand on his.

"Trust me, you'll like her," she said. "Even if you don't want to like her, you'll like her. You won't have a choice. You were literally *made* for each other."

"But that's the problem…"

Bethany took her hand away. She didn't like his new tone.

He said, "If I like her then I'll be tempted to get married. I don't want to get married. That's why I don't want to register. I was hoping that if I pushed it off long enough my matchmate would eventually move on with her life. We'd never have to meet. I would never be tempted to be with her."

"You'd rather spend your life alone?"

"It's not that I want to be alone…" Fernando had to pause to take a drink. "I just don't want to ruin the girl's life."

"Aside from not registering, how could you ruin the girl's life?"

Fernando shrugged. "I'm a Stressman. I need to fill my life with misery and sadness. There's no room to be happy. I don't want to do that to a girl. I don't want her to have to go through what Mom went through."

"So that's what this is all about? You think you'll end up like Mom and Dad?"

"People in my profession shouldn't marry. If Dad wasn't a Stressman, then maybe Mom…"

"What?" Bethany raised her voice. "You think Mom killed herself *because* Dad was a Stressman?"

"Of course she did."

"Dad had nothing to do with it. Mom was a chronically depressed person long before she met Dad. Just ask Grandma. They were perfect for each other because Dad was a Stressman."

"But I don't want a relationship like theirs."

"Well, maybe you weren't meant to be a Stressman. Did you ever think of that?"

Fernando didn't respond to that question.

"You were suspended from work," she said. "You keep complaining about not being as good a Stressman as Dad. Maybe you've chosen the wrong path in life." She pushed the paperwork closer to him. "Go to the Matchmaking Bureau tomorrow. Meet your matchmate. Perhaps she'll help put you on the right course."

Fernando looked at the papers for a second. Then put them back down and drunkenly shook his head. "No. I'm a Stressman. I don't want to get married."

Bethany stood from her seat. "Then explain to her that you don't want to get married. You owe that much to her." Then she stormed out of the bar.

Fernando ordered himself another drink and used the paperwork as a coaster. In order to get his sister off his back, he would make his appointment at the Matchmaking Bureau. But if the girl he was supposedly destined to spend his life with wanted to meet him, she was sorely mistaken. The most she was going to get out of him was a phone call.

CHAPTER THREE
MATCHMATES

Centuries ago, human beings had the ability to mate with anyone they wanted to, even those they didn't particularly like. They didn't have matchmates back then. The closest concept to a matchmate was someone they called a soulmate—the one person you were destined to be with. Very few people ever found their soulmates during their lifetime. So few, in fact, that the idea of soulmates was more of a myth. Those who thought there was one perfect person they were destined to be with were only destined for disappointment.

But over time, mankind evolved in a very peculiar way. Men and women became incapable of breeding with anyone other than their intended soulmate. This was because there was a change in the shape of human genitalia. The penis evolved into the shape of a key. The vagina had taken the form of a lock. And every one of them had a unique configuration. So there was only one male for every female, only one key that fit each lock.

Fernando Mendez, after twelve years of putting it off, was finally going to see which lock his key was designed for. He was in the lobby of the Matchmaking Bureau—a centuries-old organization that was in the business of finding people's matchmates. Fernando couldn't wait to get it all over with. He cursed his sister for putting him through such a humiliating ordeal.

"Wait… what exactly do you want me to do?" Fernando asked, holding up the bucket of putty.

The lady with the orange curly hair rolled her eyes at

Fernando and let out a patronizing groan. She had been nice to all the young men and women who were in line before him, but she became a complete bitch the second she saw Fernando. Perhaps it was because he was a decade older than everyone else registering. Many people in modern society hated those who, as they say, "hide their keys."

"How many times do I have to repeat myself?" she said, tapping her long sparkly nails on her desk. "Take these pills, then—"

"Wait, you didn't say anything about pills before?"

She took a small paper cup of pills from behind her desk and handed them to Fernando, glaring at him as if it were his fault she forgot to give them to him. "They make sure you keep an erection during the molding process."

"When do they kick in?"

"If you came in when you were younger you probably wouldn't have needed the pills."

"That didn't answer my question."

"Once your erection is set, place your key into the molding bucket. Wait an hour until the putty hardens. Then go see the doctor to get it cut off."

"You cut it off?"

She rolled her eyes again. "Just the mold. Not your key, of course."

Fernando looked down at the bucket of putty. "Of course..."

A doctor guided Fernando to a private room where he could create the mold, but the room turned out to be not quite as private as he'd been led to believe. It was full of naked guys, sitting in a circle with putty buckets on their crotches.

"Great..." Fernando said.

There was something awkward about sitting in a room with a bunch of naked guys with erections, especially when you're the only one in the group who felt awkward about it.

The other guys, all college-aged, sat back and relaxed as if they were in a sauna, watching porn on the television screen in the corner.

Fernando sat down on a bench between two large sweaty guys and took his pants down to his knees. That was as naked as he planned to get. His erection didn't come right away. He had to just sit there, holding the bucket in his lap, pretending he had his penis inside the putty. It was too awkward to sit there without the bucket in his lap.

"That bitch's lock looks tight, yo," said the teen sitting next to Fernando as they watched the porn film on the screen. "I'd unlock the shit out of that."

Fernando didn't make eye contact with him.

"I bet my bitch is going to be even hotter than her," the kid continued. "I just know I'm gonna be matched with a hottie. She'll have an amazing rack for sure."

Fernando felt sorry for whichever girl turned out to be that kid's matchmate.

A lot of young men went to the Matchmaking Bureau as soon as they turned eighteen because they thought it was a surefire way to get laid. This guy was obviously one of them. He was obviously a virgin.

"She's going to be begging for it," the teen said.

Fernando tuned him out and watched the television screen. The porn film didn't do much for him. Most porn films didn't do much for him. The women in the film stroked the men's large, bulging keys, rubbing the key shafts between their breasts, rubbing their clits at the top of their locks. It all seemed boring and mechanical.

Whenever non-matchmates, such as those in porn films, attempted sexual intercourse it was usually pretty messy and unsatisfying. Sometimes non-matched keys could fit partially into a lock, but it was a lot of uncomfortable bumping and rubbing that didn't do much for either party. Anal intercourse and oral sex was the most common method to relieve sexual tension for couples who were not matched. They called non-matched relationships *practice couplings*—temporary flings for passing time before one finds their true matchmate.

"I hope my bitch is already in the system," the teen said. "I wanna do some fucking *tonight*."

Fernando hoped the kid's matchmate turned out to be a lesbian.

Most of the time, lesbians were matched with homosexuals, and bisexuals were matched with bisexuals. These unions often resulted in foursome families, where couples of one sexual orientation would join with another, producing children with two mothers and two fathers. But every once in a while a lesbian was matched with a straight male. When such a thing occurred, people questioned whether or not a matchmate really was a person's perfect mate. But those who had researched such unions always came to the same conclusion—one of the two people in the relationship was denying their true nature.

When the medication finally kicked in, Fernando lifted his bucket and looked down at his key-shaped erection. All penis-keys had unique contours, but Fernando's had a particularly abnormal form. His key had a curved shape, like a flesh-colored stingray swimming down the head of his dick. He'd never seen a curvy key before. Most keys he'd seen in porn films or photographs looked more like ancient door keys, with square-like configurations sticking out of one side of the tip.

He pressed his key deep into the cold putty. Then he sat there and waited, trying not to make eye contact with any of the naked guys sitting across from him.

When the putty was dry, a doctor cut it off of him, scanned the mold, and uploaded it into their system. He also had to upload a lot of Fernando's personal information into the system—information he didn't really want on there. Women legally had the right to access all personal information on their matchmates, from medical records to elementary school report cards. You were left completely vulnerable to them.

Fernando heard hundreds of horror stories about guys like him who refused to marry their matchmates. Their mates would stalk them, lurk outside their homes, follow them to work, trying to wear them down until they finally gave in. And the worst part about it was that the majority of society was all in favor of this kind of stalking. They believed the crazy men and women who resorted to stalking were the victims in these circumstances. Those who refused to start a family with their matchmates were the ones in the wrong.

"How long will it take to find my match?" Fernando asked.

The doctor chewed on the end of his pen as he typed the information into the system. "If she's in the system it shouldn't take long. Just let me finish typing you up."

Fernando waited patiently. He felt a little guilty once he found himself praying his matchmate was dead, but not that guilty. It would've made his life a lot easier if he didn't have to break a woman's heart.

"And... you've got a match!" the doctor said, once the data search was complete.

Fernando didn't respond. The doctor could tell by the look on his face that he didn't really care.

"Don't get too excited..." the doctor said.

"Is she still alive?"

"She sure is."

Fernando sunk into his seat.

The doctor was about to print out her information for Fernando, but something caught his attention. His eyes locked onto the screen. "Wait a minute..."

"What's wrong?" Fernando asked.

"This has got to be some kind of error..."

"What?"

"Let me get a network specialist in here," the doctor said, stepping away from his desk. "I think we got a false match. Just wait here a minute. This happens occasionally."

Fernando tapped his foot, wondering what the holdup was. The doctor returned with a woman from the tech department who sat down behind the computer and ran a diagnostic.

"There's nothing wrong with the network," said the technician. "It looks like the right match."

"But it can't be the right match," said the doctor, who leaned over the woman's shoulder to take another look.

Fernando was getting worried. "What's wrong?"

The doctor raised his finger at him. "Just a minute."

Fernando stayed quiet, trying to remain patient.

The technician shrugged. "I don't know what to say. There's nothing else I can do."

She stood up from the desk and looked at Fernando, "Sorry."

Fernando didn't know if the *sorry* was because she couldn't solve the problem with the doctor's computer or if it was to console him for the match. She left the room as quickly as she could.

The doctor printed some papers. His hands were clearly shaking. "I have to examine the molds myself. I don't trust the computers today. Sorry for the inconvenience."

Then he left again.

After an hour of waiting around in the doctor's office, trying to listen in on the many conversations between doctors that sprung up in the hallway, Fernando was finally told what was going on. The doctor sat down in his desk and faced Fernando with a very serious expression on his face.

"I don't know how to tell you this," the doctor said. "It's something that's never happened before."

The doctor paused with his mouth open, trying to form the words.

"What?" Fernando said.

"In the three-hundred-year history of the Matchmaking Bureau, a match like this has never emerged. You're the first."

"Should I be concerned?"

Fernando was noticeably concerned.

The doctor pressed his lips together tightly, not sure how to respond to the question.

"Just spit it out," Fernando said. "Who's my match?"

"It's not exactly a *who*," the doctor said. "It's more of a *what*."

"A what?"

"I'm sorry. I shouldn't have described her as a *what*. She is your matchmate after all…" The doctor shook his head, trying to compose himself. "But, you see, the person you've been matched with isn't exactly human."

"If she's not a human then what the hell is she? A dog? A rhino?" "No," the doctor said. "She's an Ectoparasite."

Fernando froze in his seat.

"A tick?" Fernando cried.

"We've gone through the results a hundred times and there's no error. For some reason, your human key was designed for a tick woman."

"Are you messing with me?" Fernando cried. "How is that even possible?"

"I have no idea. Humans and tick people are supposed to have compatible DNA, but a matching like this is completely unprecedented. It's actually pretty amazing if you think about it."

"But aren't Ectoparasites full of diseases?"

The doctor shook his head. "No, no. That's just a myth. They sometimes carry the diseases if the beasts they infest are diseased, but Old Gloomy is disease-free. If you want to be on the safe side, you should get her cleaned up before bringing her home with you."

"I'm not bringing her home with me."

"Either way, it would be perfectly safe for you two to be together… if you choose to be together."

Fernando took some deep breaths. "I think I'm going to be sick."

The doctor went to his printer. "Let me print her information out for you, just in case you need it. We don't collect as much information from Ectoparasites as we do our human customers, but at least you'll have a name and face. Since she probably doesn't have a permanent dwelling, you might have to ask around among her people."

As the doctor handed him the printout, Fernando asked, "This isn't going to be in the news is it?"

The doctor peeked out of the window.

"Umm…" the doctor said as he scanned the parking lot. "Not yet. But I might have told a few too many people already. Word spreads like wildfire in this town. I'd be surprised if the press doesn't get wind of the story by the end of the day."

"I thought you guys weren't legally allowed to reveal matchmate information to the public."

"Under normal circumstances, maybe. But this is a special case. It's history in the making."

"I don't want to make history."

"It's too late." The doctor shrugged. "You already did."

CHAPTER FOUR
PARASITES

Fernando looked down at his matchmate's papers as he walked home from the Matchmaking Bureau. Her name was Google Pockopa, a pretty common name for a tick woman. How on Earth she was supposed to be his perfect mate was beyond confusion. They were a race of mutants who evolved to feed on giant animals like Old Gloomy. In fact, Fluffville was home to one of the biggest populations of tick people in the country, because it was the only civilization that existed on the back of a dog.

As he walked home, Fernando passed a family of tick people as they burrowed into the dogflesh ground with crustacean-like claws. They had drill-like heads that dug deep into Old Gloomy's meat so that they could drink his blood. Their round, hard-shelled bodies stuck up in the air as they drank, wiggling their multiple insect legs at him. They were disgusting creatures. Like most people in the city, Fernando rarely even looked at them. He tried to block them out, pretend they didn't exist.

He locked eyes with one of them. Just for a second and then he looked away, but it was too late. When she saw him looking, she shuffled toward him.

"Can you spare some change, Mister?" the tick mother asked Fernando.

She looked at him with her hard albino skin and big silver eyes. Tick people had human faces and human genitalia, but the majority of their bodies were covered in a rock-hard exoskeleton. Creaky squirming noises came from her lower abdomen, as if her insect parts moved and twitched on their own.

"I'm sorry," Fernando told the tick lady.

Her children frowned up at Fernando. He patted them on their pointy heads as he walked past, but wouldn't give them anything.

The tick people lived in small huts made of dog hair. They were spread all over Old Gloomy's back, living like nomads, which was why some people referred to them as Gloomville Gypsies. Fernando never gave ticks any money because they really didn't need any. They were capable of surviving on their host animal alone. They usually only wanted money for alcohol.

Although they were once human, they were never treated as human beings. Most cities in the country wouldn't allow them within city limits. The only reason why Fluffville allowed them was because they added to Old Gloomy's misery, so the more Ectoparasites living on his back the better. If only the Fluffville citizens never had to look at the disgusting things.

As he walked away from the family of tick people, Fernando looked back at them. Although he had no intention of marrying his matchmate, no matter who she was, he still couldn't help but be upset over his pairing. It made him feel less of a person. Stressmen were supposed to be honorable men, better than the average citizen. To think he was equal to an Ectoparasite was a grave insult.

He didn't want anybody to ever find out about this, but the news van was already outside his house by the time he arrived at home.

Bethany called him the next morning, waking him from a sleep he never wanted to leave.

"So, should I even ask if you went to the Matchmaking Bureau yesterday?" Her voice was as condescending as always.

Fernando groaned into his phone, rubbing the grit out

of his eyes. He really wasn't ready to talk to his sister about it. "Do you know how early it is?"

She raised her voice. "So I'm right. You didn't go. You better pay me back every penny of that fee. Harry was already pissed I spent that money on you. Once he finds out you never even went he's going to explode."

"I went," Fernando said. But he had to say it twice before she shut up. "I did what you asked."

"Really? You know I can call the Bureau and make sure you're not lying."

"I went. I wish I didn't. I'll never forgive you for making me go there, but I went." He coughed morning phlegm from his throat. "Leave me alone about it."

"Really? You actually did it?"

Fernando sat up from his bed and stretched his arms. "Yeah."

"I didn't expect that." Her mood was almost cheery. "So who's your matchmate? Is she pretty? Did you contact her yet?"

Fernando stood up and yawned into the phone. Then he looked through his window. The reporters were still out there.

"I'm guessing you didn't see the news today," he said.

"Don't change the subject."

"I'm not changing the subject. They talked about who I was matched with on the news."

"Why would they announce that on the news? Are you matched with the mayor's daughter or something?"

"I wish…"

"Then who?"

Fernando could hear her flipping through channels through the phone, looking for some sign of her brother on the local stations.

"You really don't want to know."

The sister found a channel that was showing the outside of Fernando's house. "Hey, you're on live."

Fernando looked outside and saw a camera pointing at him.

"Hey, there you are!" his sister said as she saw his head

peeking out of his window on the television.

Fernado hid inside and pushed the curtain closed so tight that not even a pinhole of light could shine through. Then he realized he should get clothed straight away.

"So what's this all about?" Bethany asked.

Fernando decided to tell her before the news got a chance to.

"My matchmate isn't human," he said, pulling his pants on.

"What?"

"I was matched with one of those Ectoparasites."

His sister went silent. She was listening more intently on what they were saying on the news.

"It's disgusting, embarrassing, and I have no idea how it's even possible, but it's true. My matchmate is a tick woman."

"You can't marry a tick!" Bethany cried.

"Of course I won't marry her."

"Promise me you won't marry her."

"I don't even want to marry a human."

"This is horrible. I'm so sorry…" She was almost in tears. She seemed more upset about it than Fernando. It was as if he told her that he had a terminal disease.

"You should be. It's your fault."

"How is it my fault?"

"You made me go to the Matchmaking Bureau."

"So? It's not my fault you got matched with a tick. You're the freak with the Ectoparasite-shaped key."

"But I would have never known if you didn't force me to go."

"Fine. It's my fault. But what are you going to do about it?"

"I'm not doing anything about it. I'm hiding in my room."

"But they're making fun of you on the news. They're talking as if you're already married to the woman and creating sketches of what your children might look like."

"I don't care. I just want everyone to leave me alone."

"You have to tell them you have no intention of marrying the tick woman."

"I already did. They don't care."

"Look, I have to go to work," Bethany said. "Don't give anyone a reason to believe that you have the slightest desire to marry the creature. And whatever you do don't go to see her."

"I have no intention of going to see her."

"I'm serious. Avoid her completely."

"I will."

For a week, Fernando was hassled by reporters from all over the world, asking him dozens of questions about how they will live together and what he thinks it will be like to be married to the mutant creature. But the story eventually went cold when he refused to meet his matchmate or divulge any information about her. When their vans drove away and everyone stopped trying to talk to him about his pairing, he thought the whole ordeal was finally over. He could finally go back to his old life. Things would be normal again. But things weren't normal. Nothing about his pairing was normal.

Once he was alone, he couldn't stop thinking about her. He couldn't stop pondering why he was chosen to breed with a parasite. What horrible thing did he do in his past to give him such bad luck. It was better for him, he knew, to be matched with somebody he had no desire to be with. The temptation to marry her was out of the question. Not even his sister would urge him to start a family now. But, still, the fact that his matchmate wasn't human made him more curious about her than he was before going to the Matchmaking Bureau. He wondered who she was or what she was like. Was she the most disgusting mutant in Gloomville or was she more human than other tick people? He wanted to know what made her his perfect match.

He realized that he had to meet her. Just once. Whether he liked it or not, she was a part of him. They were two parts of the same whole, as they always say. He needed to know what she looked like. He needed to know where she lived and what her life was like as an Ectoparasite. The curiosity was too great. All he had to do was meet her once, even if he just saw her from a distance, then his curiosity would be satisfied. Then he would be able to move on.

He didn't know where she lived since the gypsy-like parasites didn't have addresses, but he knew where the largest population of Ectoparasites lived. There was a place known as The Cluster high on Old Gloomy's neck where a densely populated community of tick people could be found. Some tick people lived there for generations, eating and breeding beneath Gloomy's patches of hair, only departing from the area once in their lifetime to be tested in the Ectoparasite branch of the Matchmaking Bureau.

When Fernando left his home, he found himself shaking. He was nervous, but he wasn't sure exactly why. It could have been due to the fact that he had to go to a side of town that most humans avoided. The Cluster was considered the worst slum of Fluffville and one of the most dangerous areas in town. Ectoparasites were known to attack humans that entered their territory, especially when in close vicinity to one of their nests. They also hassled humans for money and on some occasions mugged them for their belongings.

But that wasn't Fernando's biggest fear. He was also nervous about meeting his matchmate. There was a strange anticipation that was making him sick to his stomach, the kind of anticipation that everyone felt when they were about to meet their matchmates. He was nervous about what he would say to the tick woman if he actually spoke to her. He had to come up with a good reason why he didn't want to be with her. He didn't want to feel like a jerk and tell her that she was too ugly and disgusting to be with.

He was also afraid of what would happen if he actually was attracted to her in some strange way. They had human faces so it was possible that she was pretty.

He really hoped she wasn't pretty.

CHAPTER FIVE
THE CLUSTER

"I'm looking for this woman," Fernando said to the first tick man he came across as he entered The Cluster, holding up a picture of his matchmate.

The old insect looked at Fernando, then at the picture. Then he spewed a gray fluid down his wiry black beard. The tick man didn't speak English. Not many ticks spoke English, especially those that lived in The Cluster.

"Have you seen her?" Fernando asked.

The old tick man spewed more fluid, spraying a metallic odor into Fernando's face. It was so pungent he had to back away. Ectoparasites had their own strange language that they spoke. It was not comprised of words, it was a language of smells. They communicated by spraying fluids from glands growing on various parts of their bodies, each smell communicating a different expression. The stronger the smell, the louder they spoke.

Fernando had no idea what the old tick man was saying, but because the words were so odorous he could tell that he was practically yelling at him. When Fernando stepped away from the cranky insect, the creature turned and scuttled away like a crab.

"I'm sorry…" Fernando said, but he had no idea what he was apologizing for.

As he walked through The Cluster, it was like he was in another world. Gloomy's hair grew tall on this side of town, like he was walking through a brown forest. There were no streets or sidewalks, just soft fleshy ground dotted by hundreds of boulder-sized scabs. Everywhere Fernando looked, there were small huts made of fur. And the population was dense. Thousands of tick people surrounded him. Many were upside-down with their heads buried into the dogflesh, their butts sticking straight into the air. Others were up in the hair-trees, clutching onto them like lice, as if trying to get away from the overpopulated neighborhood below.

Everywhere he went, Fernando was attacked by clouds of aromatic speech. He couldn't tell if the tick people were trying to speak to him or if they were having conversations with each other. His skin crawled whenever he touched them, their thick beetle-like shells rubbing a greasy stink into his clothes, their spiky insect limbs cutting scratches into his soft human flesh.

They spewed harsh smell-words at him whenever he asked them about his matchmate. After an hour of this, his clothes were coated in all sorts of fragrant conversations. He wondered if tick people knew the history of each other's conversations based on the smells they carried with them. It must've been impossible for them to cheat on their wives.

Only a few ticks he came across could actually speak English, but they couldn't help him at all. There were so many Ectoparasites in that area of town that they couldn't possibly all know each other. But for some reason, he was never discouraged. He was disgusted with every step he took in The Cluster and couldn't wait until he could finally leave, but he was patient. He didn't mind how long it took. He was not going to stop looking until he found the creature he was matched with.

There was just one woman who recognized the picture. She was older and more intelligent than the other tick people in the neighborhood and could speak English fluently. Outside of her hair-hut, which was only large enough for her to squeeze her body into when she needed to sleep, she stared at him, twitching her antennae back and forth. She said the woman in the photo was one of her thirty-six living daughters.

"You're the man the reporters told me about," said the old tick woman.

Her human face was wrinkled and covered in dried dog blood. Her exoskeleton was also wrinkled; it was gray and brittle, almost soggy. She smelled diseased and rotten. She was the most disgusting tick woman he'd ever met. He couldn't believe that she was the mother of his perfect mate.

"Yeah, how did you know?"

"They came here looking for my daughter as you came to look for her."

Fernando was thrown off by what she just said. He had no idea the reporters knew who his matchmate was. They'd been trying to get that information out of him for days. He wondered if one of them secretly paid somebody at the Matchmaking Bureau to give up that information.

"What did you tell them?"

"Nothing. Just as I'm going to tell you nothing."

She squirted a noxious cloud of bile at him, as if cursing him in her native tongue. Fernando had coughed and choked on her odor, then stepped back and covered his mouth.

"I think it's sick that you were matched with my daughter," she told him. "It's unnatural. Our kind should never be paired in such a way. We were not meant to interbreed."

Fernando coughed and waved her stink away.

"I agree," he said. "I don't want to be matched with her either. I just want to meet her and explain to her why we shouldn't be together."

The tick lady squinted at Fernando. "No, you're lying. I can tell."

"I'm not lying."

"Your human words tell me one thing but your smells tell me another," she said.

"I don't smell."

"It's very faint, but I can read your human smells. They are not much different than our smells, only you speak in muffled whispers. Your smells are saying that you want a mate."

Fernando shook his head at her. "I don't care what my smells are saying. I don't want a mate. And if I did, it wouldn't be with a filthy bug."

She flared at him with her cold eyes and raised a pincher at him in an almost threatening way.

"My daughters are not filthy bugs," she said.

Fernando tried not to offend her again. "I'm sorry. She's not a filthy bug. The point is I don't want to have anything to do with her. I just want to meet her once and then I'll never see her again."

"You can live without meeting her."

"Have you told her about me yet? Does she know a human is her matchmate?"

"No," she said. "I don't plan to tell her anything. She will never know a human is her matchmate."

"But don't you think she would want to know? It would be cruel for her to go her whole life wondering who her matchmate is."

"It's better she never knows than end up forming a vile union with you."

"I agree, but that will never happen. I promise."

Fernando couldn't believe he was arguing so much. He didn't know why he was so desperate to meet his tick matchmate. He wondered if what the woman smelled on him was true, maybe he did have some kind of deep instinctual urge to mate with something, anything, even a filthy bug, and he just didn't realize it. But, more likely, she was just sensing his sexual repression. He hadn't had sex with anyone for years and rarely even masturbated. Anyone could tell that he was in need of sexual release. But that didn't mean anything. He'd rather relieve the tension through masturbation than sex with an insect. Or he'd rather do what lonely old perverts did and cut a penis-sized hole in the warm meat ground and fuck that. Though it was something he would never actually do, it was still preferable to having sex with a tick woman.

He paused, changed his voice to a calmer tone, then said, "Look, I just want to meet her and get it over with. I need closure. Otherwise, I'm worried she might show up on my doorstep someday. All she has to do is go to the Matchmaking Bureau and they'll tell her where I live."

The old woman paused for a moment to think about that.

Fernando continued, "She'll find out eventually. There's nothing you can do to stop that. Don't you think it would be better to get it over with now?"

The woman frowned and sprayed a potato-bug odor at him, as if she hated that she couldn't come up with an argument for him.

"You're not going to stop until you find her, are you?" she asked.

"Nope. I have all the time in the world."

"And you swear that you don't want to be with her? No matter what your smells say?"

"After I meet her, I have no intention of ever speaking to her again. No offense, but I'd rather die than marry your daughter."

"Good," she said. "Because I, too, would rather you die than marry my daughter. And I'll make sure that happens if I ever see the two of you together after this day."

Fernando nodded in agreement. "So you're going to tell me where I can find her?"

"I'll tell you where she lived the last time I saw her five years ago."

"She doesn't live in The Cluster?"

"Not since she was a teenager."

It was dark by the time Fernando finally found Google Pockopa, his parasitic matchmate. She lived far away from other Ectoparasites, in the art district on Old Gloomy's lower back. Her hut made of dog hair was similar to the one her mother lived in, but it was placed between two dumpsters, in an alley behind a record shop.

"Hello?" Fernando asked as he entered the alleyway.

It was where her mother said Google would be. The old woman mentioned that her daughter lived there because she liked listening to the music that issued from the record shop next door, swaying to the classical violin concertos they played in the morning and tapping her crustacean-like claws to the bouncy pop music they played in the afternoon. It was like a hobby to her, which her mother felt was a bit eccentric since most tick people didn't have hobbies outside of eating and breeding.

"Hello?" Fernando called out again. "I'm looking for Google Pockopa."

He didn't see anyone in the alley, but he could tell the tick woman was still living there. He found her hair-hut between the dumpsters. The ground was covered in scabs and mounds of black crusty feces.

"Are you here? Your mother told me where I could find you."

Then he saw her hiding behind the corner, peeking out at him. Her antennae wiggling like curious puppy tails.

"I wanted to meet you," he said.

She ducked behind the wall when he stepped closer.

"I'm not going to hurt you."

When he went around the corner to see her, she curled inward like a roly-poly, closing herself up inside her outer shell to protect her soft human parts. She had paint sprayed on her back, dents and scars covering the insect sections of her body. It was obvious that she'd been abused. He imagined it had to be the work of hooligan teenagers who probably went into her alley and threw rocks at her for fun.

"Are you okay?" he asked.

She flinched at his words and hid deeper into her shell. As he examined her wounded body, Fernando became more and more angry at what had been done to her. He wanted to find those street kids and throw rocks at them, show them what it felt like to be hurt in such a horrible way. But, as he had these thoughts, he was surprised that he was so offended. He knew she was just a pathetic bug, she was just trash, no better than a stray dog. But, still, somewhere deep inside he knew she was a part of him. And it pissed him off knowing that somebody had been hurting a part of him.

"I've come to talk to you," he said. He pulled out his papers from the Matchmaking Bureau and showed them to her. "For some strange reason, we've been matched."

As he held out the papers, she peeked out of her shell. She looked confused, but he wasn't sure if she was confused by what he said or if she was confused that he was a human who didn't want to beat her. She squirted a pine-flavored scent at him.

"I'm your matchmate."

As Fernando said this, she looked at the paper and then looked up at him. She didn't seem to be able to speak English, she couldn't read the words printed on the paper, but she still recognized her file from the Matchmaking Bureau. She understood what it meant.

"Mate?" she asked.

Her voice was slow and crackly, like that of a deaf woman. It was obvious she didn't use her human vocal chords very often. She only knew a few words.

"Yes," Fernando said. "We're matchmates."

As Fernando said this, she opened her shell and a warm, buttery aroma drifted toward him. It was a comforting, welcoming smell. He had no idea what she was trying to say with that smell, but if he had to guess he'd say she was expressing how happy she was that she finally found her home. Obviously, he didn't like it.

"My name is Fernando Mendez," he said.

Then he paused. She stood up, her shell wide open, coming closer to him to investigate the human she was matched with. Now that she was exposed, he could finally get a good look at her. She was definitely different from other Ectoparasites, but not at all more human. Her head was round instead of drill-shaped, like she was wearing an exoskeleton helmet with antennae sticking out the top. Her skin was softer and paler than that of a normal tick woman, probably from living in a dark alleyway where the sun never shined.

"Mentis," she said, trying to repeat his name.

Her face was not very pretty. Fernando was happy for that. He didn't know what he would do if he thought she had a pretty face. Because she didn't have human hair or makeup, she didn't look very feminine and Fernando was only attracted to the most feminine women. Although she had sexy, heart-shaped lips and big dark brown eyes, he thought she looked too much like a little boy. He hated women that had that little boy look to them.

However, though she didn't have a pretty face Fernando still felt attracted to her—or at least parts of her. She had unusually large breasts for a tick woman, breasts that seemed to ooze out of her shell, dangling over her insect appendages, the kind of breasts that you could only find in Japanese comic books. Although they were white as paper with nearly invisible areolas, he couldn't take his eyes off of them. They didn't seem to belong on such a disgusting insect body.

"I've only come to tell you that we were matched," Fernando told her as she wiggled her antennae at him. "But I'm not interested in being with you. I just wanted to meet you and let you know that I don't want to form a relationship."

She discharged gray fluids from her lower abdomen, releasing more of the buttery smell. The closer she got to him, the stronger the scent. They were trying to communicate with each other, but neither knew what the other was saying.

"I'm sorry, but I have no interest in starting a family, especially not with a…" Fernando lost himself as she looked at him with her dark brown eyes. "Anyway, I thought you should know, just in case you were waiting for your matchmate all these years. You can finally move on."

He could tell what he was saying wasn't getting through to her. She sprayed him with a sweet flowery tequila odor. It was almost flirtatious.

"How do I explain myself…" he said.

Then he looked her in the eyes again and realized meeting this woman was a terrible mistake. He could tell she was desperate. She had been all alone for so long, treated horribly by humans and probably treated as a freak by her own kind due to her unusual features. The excited look in her eyes was not only because she'd finally found her mate, but because she'd found her hero—the person who would take her away from her life of misery. It was so pathetic that he couldn't help but feel like such a horrible person for not being willing to give her what she so desperately needed.

"We can't be together," he said. Then he thought of the one word he knew that she understood. "No mate. Do you understand? No mate."

"Matchmate…" she said.

She grabbed his arms with her crustacean-like pinchers, almost like she was trying to hug him. The warm, buttery smell oozed out of her skin and soaked into his t-shirt as she pressed herself against him.

"No," Fernando said. "No matchmate."

He pushed away from her and shook his head, trying to get her to understand that he was rejecting her. She just stared at him, unable or unwilling to understand. Fernando looked down at her vagina. He didn't want to, but curiosity got the better of him. He wanted to know how it was even possible for her lock to be the perfect match for his key. Her vagina was on the insect part of her body. It was a dark crusty mucus-filled hole on her lower abdomen. He couldn't believe that his human penis could possibly be shaped to unlock it. Just the idea of it was disgusting. He was beginning to feel sick.

But as he imagined turning his key inside of that foul crispy hole, he found himself getting erect. It was out of his control. Something inside of him didn't care if her lock was disgusting. It was designed for him. It was his nature to want to unlock her.

The tick woman saw his erection and tried to wrap her claws around him again, but he pushed her away. This confused her. He was giving her mixed signals. His body was asking her to embrace him, but his words and actions were refusing her. She didn't know how to respond.

"Matchmate or no matchmate?" she asked.

Fernando held up the papers and ripped them in half.

"No matchmate," he said. He tossed the papers aside and broke eye contact with her. "I'm sorry."

She sprayed him with a toxic, eggy musk. He waved the smell away. It was so strong it burned his eyes. Based on her facial expression, he didn't think the smell meant she was angry at him for his response. It seemed like she was begging him to reconsider, perhaps asking him *but don't you want to have children someday?*

To whatever she said, he shook his head no one last time. Then he turned around and walked out of the alley. He didn't look back. He just left, trying to hide his erection from the people outside the record shop.

CHAPTER SIX
THE STRAY

It took seven blocks before Fernando realized that the tick woman was following him.

"Go back," Fernando said. "I don't want you."

She stopped, but she did not turn back, wiggling her insect appendages at him. When he turned around to move forward, she continued following him.

"No," he told her. "Go back. No."

"Home…" she said.

"No home," he yelled. "I don't want you going to my home."

After spending so many days being hassled by reporters, the last thing he wanted was to have anyone see a tick woman around his house. If one of his neighbors saw her, they'd probably get the media back on his doorstep within the hour.

"Go away."

But she didn't listen. She was persistent. He wished he didn't get aroused when he was around her. By doing that, it probably convinced her that she still had a chance to be with him. It made her think that part of him was looking for a mate.

"I said go away!"

Fernando picked up a rock and threw it at her. She flinched and closed up her shell, but the rock didn't come anywhere near where she stood. He didn't want to hurt her. He just wanted to scare her away. It didn't work.

He moved forward a few feet. Whenever he found a rock, he would pick it up and throw it at her. She would hide in her shell for a moment. But once he turned around, she would come out of her shell and hurry after him. After a while, Fernando stopped throwing rocks. Not only because it did not prove effective, but also because it was very difficult to find rocks on top of a giant dog. The rocks he did find were mostly just chunks of asphalt.

"Are you going to follow me all the way home?" he asked.

She wiggled her antennae.

Fernando shook his head and moved on. He tried to pick up his pace, move faster down the road. But Google picked up her pace as well. She scuttled as fast as she could on her six insect legs, shuffling down the road so that she wouldn't lose Fernando. At first, she was able to keep up. But then Fernando went even faster. He ran at top speed, rushing through the streets as though running from certain death, not looking back for even a second as he escaped the hideous mutant.

It was an hour after he got home when he heard the scratching on his front door. He looked out the window to see her insect shell shifting and oozing with strange fluids. Through the door, he could smell the warm, buttery odor leaking out of her at full strength.

"How the hell did she find me?"

Fernando had lost her. He ran far faster than she could keep up. There was no way she would have been able to find him.

"Mentis?" she said on the other side of the door.

He realized she must have followed his scent. He probably left a scent trail all the way to his house. Either it was his own body smells or maybe she had marked him with a special odor she could follow. Whatever the case, she'd found him and unless he moved far away she would always be able to find him.

"Mentis?" she repeated in her awkward human voice.

He opened the door. She scuttled forward, as if trying to squeeze her way inside, but Fernando left the door open only a crack. He would not allow her entry.

"I told you to go away," he said.

She wouldn't go away. She oozed a glue-like smell, as if trying to convince him to give her a chance.

"I find you repulsive," he said. "Don't you find me repulsive, too? We're not the same species. We should not be together."

She continued oozing different smells, as if speaking as fast as she could. Fernando wasn't dealing with a normal woman. Humans could be reasoned with. They have intelligence and the ability to resist their primal urges most of the time. But Ectoparasites had very little intelligence. They possessed insect-like brains and were driven purely by instinct. All they cared about was eating and breeding. It wasn't going to be easy for him to convince her to leave.

"Look, you need to go," he said, shaking his head as he spoke. "You can't stay here."

She sprayed him with more smells, so many that his senses were overwhelmed and they all blurred together into one.

"I don't want any of my neighbors to see you out here."

She said, "But Mentis…"

Then she gave him a long face. He could tell she didn't want to go back to the alley where the humans constantly abused her. Even though he didn't want to have anything to do with her, he agreed that she should never go back there.

"I'm sorry," he said. "I never should have gone to see you."

She sprayed him with the buttery odor in such a strong dose that it made his head drift, his muscles loosened. The smell was like a loving embrace. It was like she was hugging him, soothing him with her words.

"Fine," he said.

He had no idea what she was saying to him with that smell, but apparently she convinced him to let her come inside.

"Get in before any of my neighbors see you out here."

She shuffled into his house like a monstrous crab, spewing a minty bologna smell at him as if thankful for letting her inside. Fernando didn't know what he was going to do about her, but he knew if he left her on his porch she would just wait out there until the news vans returned.

He decided he would let her spend the night. Then, the next day, he would visit the tick woman's mother. The old bug lady could translate for him and convince her daughter to stay away. Then the whole ordeal would finally come to an end.

Fernando was at first worried that the tick woman would misinterpret his gesture as an invitation to mate with him, but once inside she did not try anything. She was respectful. She seemed to be content with checking out what she thought was her new home.

She looked around his house, smelling at all of his furniture, investigating the place with her creepy antennae. She crawled around his carpet face-down, using all six of her insect legs. When she was down on all legs, she didn't look human at all. Her human features—face, neck, breasts, and belly—were hidden beneath her shell and all he could see was her massive insect body and wiggling antennae. It was like he had a six-foot cockroach scurrying through his home. He'd never seen anything so disgusting.

"You can sleep out here," he told her, when she sniffed her way through the living room. "We'll go see your mother in the morning."

"No eat," she said, pointing at his floor.

She seemed to be wondering how she was going to feed on Old Gloomy's blood with his floor covering the flesh-earth.

"If you have to feed you need to go in the backyard," he

said. "You can't go in the front or people will see."

She scraped her claws on the carpet, trying to dig through like a dog attempting to bury a bone.

"No," Fernando said. He pushed on her shell. "Stop it. You're tearing up the carpet."

She stopped and looked up at him, wondering why he had such a strange home that covered up the ground.

"Eat," she said.

Fernando wiped his greasy hands against his thigh. "You'll have to wait until morning."

"Eat," she said.

Fernando sighed. "Fine. Come with me."

She followed him to the other side of the house. When he opened the sliding glass door, he pointed at a bald patch of ground in the center of his fenced yard. Hair as tall as trees grew along the fence, giving him privacy from his neighbors. He had no problem with her feeding back there.

She just stood in place, looking at him with her dark brown eyes. He realized she wasn't trying to dig through the floor because she was hungry. She just wanted to know how she was going to live in a house with a covered floor. It was inconvenient for an Ectoparasite.

"Go ahead," Fernando said. "Eat."

She watched him for a few more minutes, then looked at the yard. He pointed at the bald spot of ground until she finally went outside.

"Good tick," he said.

She turned to him with a glare when he said the word tick. She must have had a bad association with the word. Those hooligan teenagers who bullied and assaulted her must have called her that word many times before. She almost seemed offended that her matchmate would use such a cruel term.

"Sorry," Fernando said. But he really didn't care too much. He wondered if she would go away if he used the term enough.

Because his matchmate didn't have a drill-shaped head, she wasn't able to dig into Old Gloomy's flesh as easily as normal parasites. She chewed into his meat with her shark-like teeth, ripped open the flesh with her claws, and then squeezed her head deep inside the hole until she could reach the blood.

As her bulbous body hovered in the air, Fernando watched her get plump with blood. He couldn't imagine the flavor of drinking dog blood. It must have tasted so rusty, so earthy. He'd heard of poor people sometimes carving chunks of flesh from the dog's back whenever they were desperate for food, but drinking the blood was even more disgusting than that.

Twenty minutes passed and the woman still didn't stop drinking. Fernando decided it would be best to leave her outside over night. He put a bowl of water out for her, as if she were some kind of stray dog. Then he turned off the lights and closed the sliding glass door.

"Goodnight," he said.

She stayed out there with her head deep inside the dogflesh, probably unaware that he locked her out as she fed. But Fernando didn't care. He went to his room and tried to go to sleep before she noticed he was gone.

In the middle of the night, Fernando dreamt that a giant cockroach was crawling on top of him, licking his neck with a forked tongue that smelled of raw shrimp. He woke to see the tick woman staring down at him in the dark, her antennae wiggling over his head.

Fernando jumped up and turned on the light.

"What are you doing in here?" he cried.

She touched him with her pincher. "Sleep…"

"You can't sleep in here," he said. "Go back outside."

Even if she understood what he was saying, she didn't listen to him. She kissed his neck, licked him with her strange tongue.

"Stop," Fernando said. But he didn't do anything to make her stop.

She used her left pincher to cut his pajama shirt, snipping it from the bottom up to the top. Then she sprayed him with the warm, buttery odor. It filled his lungs, calmed him, made him feel comfortable around her. Then she pressed her breasts against his bare chest.

He closed his eyes and tried to forget who or what she was. As she kissed him and rubbed her breasts in a circle against him, she almost seemed like a real woman. His penis grew erect.

"We shouldn't…" Fernando said.

He knew it was wrong. He knew it was the last thing he should do. But he couldn't help himself. He lifted his butt into the air so she could cut away his pajama pants.

Naked together, beneath the covers, it almost seemed normal. They were just two people touching each other, warming themselves against each other. But then the fluids came out. These weren't the same as the usual odorous communication fluids. These were sexual fluids that thickened as the tick woman became aroused.

It oozed from her breasts—an invisible grease that smelled of cooking oil—leaking down Fernando's chest and belly as she rubbed her nipples in circles against him. The fluid was like some kind of lubricant, allowing their bodies to slip and slide across each other. It even made her hard exoskeleton smoother, less abrasive.

"What the hell's wrong with me…" Fernando moaned to himself. "What the hell am I doing…"

But he couldn't pull himself away. His key was pointed at that crusty, lumpy hole in her lower abdomen and no matter how disgusting he thought it was there was a part of him that was begging to unlock it.

"We shouldn't do this…" Fernando told the insect.

But she wouldn't listen. She'd been waiting her entire life for this moment. She wasn't going to back down now.

She rubbed her insect appendages along her lower abdomen, stroking and vibrating against the wiry black hairs. It reminded Fernando of a spider spinning its web around its prey, only he assumed she was stimulating herself, getting herself ready for him.

"I think I should take a cold shower," Fernando said, trying to get out of the bed before anything really happened.

But she wouldn't let him leave. She grabbed his upper arm with her pincher, squeezing firmly yet delicately, pulling him back toward her. When she was finished rubbing her lower section, the exoskeleton swelled open like a mouth lined with black needle-like teeth. Then the mucus flowed out. It was a fishy yellowish-white substance with the consistency of tapioca pudding. It oozed out of her in baseball-sized discharges, rolling down her insect thighs and abdomen, making glugging, smacking sounds as it poured. Fernando was terrified of it, disgusted by it, but not as terrified or disgusted by the fact that it made him more aroused. He still wanted to put his key inside. He still wanted to see what it would be like.

Though the smell attacked his nose, he didn't resist as she rubbed the creamy custard across his legs and belly. He just laid back and watched as she scuttled on top of him, covering him with her shell. Then his penis disappeared into that gooey mess. At first, it was bumpy and prickly inside. It felt as though giant balls of tapioca shifted and tightened around his member.

Then the magic happened. The thing his body had been craving since the moment he laid eyes on the creature. His key went all the way inside the lock. Fernando gasped. He was surprised how much it really was a perfect fit. Every groove, every angle, every curve of his key was identical to those in her lock. It fit better than a glove. No matter how disgusting the bug woman was to him, their sex organs really were designed for each other.

Fernando felt his key turning inside of her, his foreskin moving counterclockwise around his penis, all on its own, unlocking the tick woman's vagina. When it shifted all the way around, there was a slight popping sensation. Then his key went deeper inside her body, burrowing through new

66

areas of mucus and lumpy flesh.

As they made love, Fernando lost himself in ecstasy, burying himself in the sticky grossness. Although their sex organs were a perfect fit, Fernando quickly learned that the rest of their bodies were not built to mate with each other. The tick's exoskeleton was like a baseball bat hammering Fernando's soft human skin as they thrust into each other. The wiry hairs on her lower abdomen poked him like cactus needles. Her insect legs were like crowbars wrapped in barbed wire, slicing his flesh open as she gripped him tightly. He bled, his bones were bruised, but he wouldn't stop.

He held her closely, wrapped in her thorny arms, as she curled her shell around him like a roly-poly. He couldn't see anything any more, encased in her body, buried in her moist smells. She held him safely inside of her, licking his face, wanting to be unlocked over and over again.

CHAPTER SEVEN
BROKEN HOME

In the morning, Fernando could hardly get out of his bed. It hurt to move. His body was torn up, covered in scratches, abrasions, and a few deep gashes along his inner thighs. The fishy mucus covering his body had congealed into a thick crust, gluing his body hairs together, infecting his wounds. His penis was buried under a mound of the tick woman's creamy vagina pudding. His sheets were saturated in black slime.

A variety of strong odors discharged from his bed as he sat up, as if the smells were supposed to be some kind of love letter the tick woman left for him. She was nowhere to be seen, but there were signs of her everywhere. His walls were scratched up, as if she was trying to peel down all of the wall paper. Both lamps were in pieces on the floor. A trail made of some kind of foul-smelling oily substance went from the bathroom to the bed to the bedroom door.

"What the hell…"

Fernando realized what a horrible mistake he'd made allowing the woman to enter his home. He knew he needed to get rid of her as soon as possible. There was a good reason why Ectoparasites did not live inside of human homes. They were vermin.

"Gross…"

When he saw himself in the bathroom mirror, the thick custard dangling from his key, he thought back to every little detail of the sex he had the night before. He remembered sliding his key into that black, lumpy pus sack, ignoring how disgusting it all was. But he was aroused then. Now that he was sober, the thought of what he did made him nauseous.

After puking three times into the sink, he hopped in the shower and washed the creature's stink from his body. The hot water burned away the itchiness from his wounds and melted the crust from his crotch. The water pooling in the tub below turned a dark brown. He didn't want to leave the shower. It was soothing and warm. He didn't want to have to face the tick woman again.

The rest of his house was in even worse shape than the bedroom. The sliding glass door was shattered. The walls were covered in some kind of black fluid that had hardened into a cocoon. And the living room floor was gone. The tick woman had ripped away the carpet and cracked open the concrete foundation to expose a patch of dogflesh where she could feed.

When Fernando saw the tick woman with her head buried in the floor, her abdomen in the air, he thought he was going to be sick again. He sat down on the couch, trying not to get any mucus on his clean pants, and just stared at the creature until she was finished with her breakfast.

"Are you done?" he asked.

She replied with a burnt sugar odor.

In the daylight, the tick was even more grotesque than she was the previous night. Even her human parts, her face and large breasts, were ugly to Fernando.

"Good, because we're leaving."

The tick woman went to him and wiggled her antennae. She placed a blood-wet pincher into his hand and stared at him with her big brown eyes. Then she sprayed a baked bread odor at him, which Fernando translated to mean that she was happy and never wanted to leave him.

"I'm taking you to your mother today. She agrees with me that we don't belong together. Hopefully she'll be able to talk some sense into you."

But she had no idea what she was saying. She was convinced that she had finally found her mate and would live there with him for the rest of her life. It wasn't going to be easy to get rid of her.

There was a knock at the door and Fernando leapt from his seat, pushing the tick woman away from him. She sprayed him with three angry odors as he shoved her into the bedroom. He thought for sure it was going to be the media again, assuming one of his neighbors had to have seen the Ectoparasite around his house and called the press.

But it wasn't the press. It was even worse. It was his sister.

"Fernando?" Bethany said through the door. "I know you're home. Open up."

Fernando couldn't let his sister know about the tick woman. He couldn't let her inside. But he knew her. He knew she would push her way in if he opened the door. So he left through the backyard and walked around the house to greet her out front.

"What are you doing here?" he asked, walking through his furry lawn toward her.

"I came to check up on you. What were you doing in your back yard?"

Fernando shrugged. He didn't have time for a good lie. "I was about to do some yard work. Pull weeds."

"You? Do yard work?"

"I don't have anything better to do," he said.

"That's actually why I'm here," she said, coming toward him with an envelope. "I've been worried about you ever since this matchmate business. I have no idea how I would be able to cope if I were matched with one of those disgusting things. It's just terrible."

Fernando nodded. She didn't know the half of it.

"It must be so lonely knowing that you'll never have a

mate," she said. "I know you said you never wanted to get married, but I always figured that someday you'd change your mind. Now, even if you change your mind, you'll never have a matchmate."

A strong pine odor flowed out of the front door and filled the yard. The tick woman was yelling at him, trying to ask him what the heck he was doing outside with that other woman. Fernando moved his garbage from his garage down to the end of his driveway, leading his sister away from the front door before she could smell the tick's language or hear the scratching noises coming from within.

"So I want you to meet a co-worker of mine," she said, forcing the envelope into Fernando's hand. "I think you'll like her."

He opened it up to find pictures of a stocky red-headed woman with a mousy smile. He already didn't like her. "Are you serious?"

"Her matchmate died in the earthquake last week. The one you caused by getting Old Gloomy too excited."

Fernando froze. "What are you talking about? Nobody died in that earthquake last week…"

"One person did."

"How?" Fernando couldn't believe it. He had no idea he'd been responsible for someone's death. Nobody had told him. "It was hardly even an earthquake. There wasn't even any property damage."

"He was driving to work at the time. When the ground rumbled, he thought the dog's tail was about to wag. He panicked. He tried to flee the area, going ninety-eight miles per hour. Then he lost control, crashed into the back of a garbage truck, and died in the hospital a few days later."

"But… But that wasn't my fault!" Fernando cried. "He's the one who crashed his car."

"If you hadn't messed up at work that day it never would have happened," Bethany said. "Mary, the girl I work with, was supposed to meet him the same day of the crash. She was devastated, as you can imagine."

"So you want me to meet this woman? Why? So she can tell me how I ruined her life?"

"No," Bethany said. "I want you to put her life back together. I want you to fill the void you created in her life."

"Are you saying…"

"I'm saying that I want you to marry her."

"Marry her? Why? What would be the point if I'm not her matchmate?"

"Neither of you have matchmates, so you should be together. It's better than spending the rest of your lives alone."

"But we can't have children. We don't love each other. It's stupid."

"Actually, you *can* have children together. And love can come later."

"How the heck can we have children together?"

"With an insemination device," she said. "Before her matchmate was taken off of life support, they made a silicone replica of his key and saved an ample amount of his sperm. She can use the replica like a dildo to unlock her womb and spray the semen inside. Getting pregnant won't be an issue. But she needs a father for her children."

"And you want me to be that father?"

"Yes," she said. "You caused the problem. You're going to fix it."

"But I can't be a father. I don't even have a job."

"There's a position opening up in the shipping department at my company," she said, handing him a card for the hiring manager. "Call this number. He'll set you up."

"No," Fernando said. "I'm a Stressman. I'm not working at your company."

"Wherever you work, it doesn't matter. You could be a stay at home dad for all I care. But you're meeting Mary. You're going to set things right."

"This is insane, Bethany. Even for you."

"I'm bringing her here next Thursday at seven. Be presentable."

"No way. Not going to happen."

"You said you had nothing better to do." Bethany turned and walked back to her car at the end of the driveway.

"I don't care. Don't bring her here." Fernando raised his voice, but she didn't look back. "Are you listening to me?"

Before she got in her car and drove off, she said one last thing:

"You should go take a shower. You smell like a sewer."

She was gone before he got the chance to tell her that he just got out of the shower.

When Fernando went back inside, the tick woman was spraying the house with some kind of raw hamburger odor. It was like she was leaving a warning message for all other women who entered the home. The message read: stay away.

"We're leaving within the hour," Fernando said to her.

She didn't look back at him. She seemed angry.

Fernando smelled his shirt and realized that he did smell like a sewer. He removed his clothes and took another shower. But when he smelled himself again, the tick woman's stink still saturated his skin. He took three more showers, used bar soap, dish soap, and rubbing alcohol, but nothing could remove the smell. It was like her odor penetrated his bloodstream as they had sex the night before, and now he was sweating the stuff. He wondered if it was a way that Ectoparasites tagged their mates.

Fernando waited until there was nobody outside who would see him with the tick woman. Then he left, heading in the direction of The Cluster. At first, his matchmate didn't want to leave his house. She wanted to stay, probably to mate again. So he left without her. It only took a few minutes of waiting outside before she followed.

"Let's move quickly," he said, leading her shuffling arachnid body through his neighborhood, watching to make sure nobody was looking.

When he saw a car drive by or someone in the neighborhood looking out of their window, he'd put as much distance as he could between him and the insect, ignoring her, pretending as if she was just a random Ectoparasite traveling in the same direction as he was.

"Mentis…" she said, catching up to Fernando.

She tried to open up a dialog, even though they couldn't understand each other. Based on the pine smell in the air, Fernando assumed she was confused about where he was taking her.

"This needs to end before it goes any further," he said to her. "I don't know what we'd do if you ended up getting pregnant."

As they walked, Fernando thought about the idea of impregnating a disgusting creature like the tick woman. He imagined her insect abdomen swelling with his child, then giving birth to some strange half-tick baby. The concept horrified him, yet at the same time it made him aroused. He found himself trying to cover his erection as they walked down the sidewalk.

"Mentis…" she said to him, wrapping her pincher around his waist.

The pincher was cold and hard, but somehow soothing against his skin. He wrapped his fingers around the top of the claw, feeling the smooth texture.

Her other insect appendages wrapped around his hips and stopped him in his tracks.

"Home," she said to him, peering into his eyes.

The buttery smell filled his nostrils as his penis grew even harder, digging into the shell of her lower abdomen. As her breasts squished into his arms, her lips widened with rapid breaths, Fernando couldn't control himself any longer.

"Let's go," he said.

Then he led her back to his house, snuck her inside, and took her into the bedroom. They made love for hours, oozing into each other, covering each other with stink and slime. Fernando wanted to resist. He wanted to kick her out of the bed, shove her out of the house, but something inside of him wouldn't allow that. It wanted nothing more than to be inside of her, to be covered by her creamy eggy fluids.

They weren't meant to live together, they weren't meant to be a part of the same society, they weren't even meant to communicate, but there was one thing they were meant for. And as the tick woman squirmed and clawed at his flesh, pumping in and out with gooey squirts, Fernando realized that he couldn't get enough of it.

That was, until they finished. Then Fernando hated himself, and he hated her, with all of his soul. He wished he never would have brought her back. He wished he could have taken her to The Cluster and ditched her there for good.

CHAPTER EIGHT
HIVE

For several days, Fernando gave up on the world and allowed his instincts to take over. He made love with the tick woman many times a day, not bothering to even take a shower anymore, allowing her cream-colored mucus to harden across his chest and legs. Immediately after orgasm, he'd always push off of her and run to the bathroom to throw up, then he'd curse himself in the mirror for being such a disgusting pervert for enjoying it so much.

His house didn't look like the same place anymore. It had been transformed by the insect woman. Without the flooring in place, his living room was beginning to grow fur between the mounds of scab left behind after his matchmate's feedings. The ground was covered in her black, charcoal-like shit that Fernando had to scoop out with a shovel every morning. The walls and ceilings became covered in a thick cocoon, transforming the appearance of his house into the domain of an insect. Fernando felt as if he was now living inside of a giant beehive.

Fernando had seen the nests the Ectoparasites made on the surface, which looked very similar to the cocooned walls of his home. But they were very small, the size of a garbage can or a tractor tire at the biggest. He'd never seen an Ectoparasite nest as large as the one that was being built inside of his home. Because of this, Fernando refused to believe the tick woman was actually building a nest at all. He kidded himself into thinking it was what tick people did to the insides of their homes. He'd never actually been inside of an Ectoparasite's hair-hut before. It would make sense they would want to cocoon the interior of their huts in order to keep out the rain and insulate for warmth.

But Fernando realized he was just deluding himself once the tick woman began laying eggs. One morning, he saw a pile of the mucus-covered white orbs in the corner of the living room, but thought nothing of them at first. He assumed they were just some kind of strange insect discharge. But then he saw the insect woman in the bathroom, squatting over the bathtub, squirting out the same gooey eggs into the basin. A putrid fishy odor filled the bathroom as the tick stared blankly at Fernando, squeezing out egg after egg.

"Eggs?" he cried. "Are you fucking serious?"

She didn't respond. Her lower insect limbs twitched and quivered, rubbing a yellow pudding across her lower abdomen to lubricate the birthing process.

Fernando ran out of the room and fell to his knees on the hairy living room floor. He looked at the egg pile in the corner. It made him so sick he was shaking. Reality came crashing in. Although he was having sex with the tick woman, which was disgusting enough on its own, it didn't really dawn on him that he'd been breeding with her. He kept telling himself that he could get rid of her at any time, that he didn't have to marry her, that he could just have sex for a while and then his life would one day go back to normal. But these eggs… These were his children. These were permanent. If he allowed the eggs to hatch he would never be able to go back to his old life. He would have to tell his sister about his relationship with the tick, the news stations would eventually find out, his boss, his neighbors. His life would be over.

When he was a kid, he had friends who would sneak into Ectoparasite nests and steal their eggs. Then they would smash them against walls, throw them at cars, stomp on them until they were chunky pools of goo. Fernando knew it was cruel, but it was something that most human kids did when they were at that destructive age. It wasn't exactly illegal to smash tick eggs. The reason they laid so many was because tick mothers expected to lose the majority of their young, since the eggs were often destroyed by seagulls, rats, stray dogs, and even other Ectoparasites who saw neighboring nests as competition.

Fernando didn't have a choice. Deep inside of his soul a part of him cried out, begging him to stop. But his logical brain knew this was what had to be done. He couldn't allow the freaks to be born. He smashed every egg in the living room with a shovel. Then he went in the bathroom, locked the tick woman out, and destroyed every egg in the tub.

Google cried, filling the air with a desperate vinegar scent, furiously trying to scratch her way through the door as her babies were smashed to a pulp. She couldn't understand why her mate would do such a horrible thing. She wondered if she'd done something wrong.

Fernando hated himself for it. He screamed with every strike of the shovel, cursing himself, fighting every instinct in his body in order to get the job done. When it was over, Fernando opened the bathroom door and pushed his way past the tick woman as raisin-scented tears flowed down her cheeks. He didn't care if she hated him for what he did. If she hated him maybe she would leave him, then all of his problems would be solved.

Google began hiding her eggs from Fernando. She'd lay them in secret, while he was sleeping. He'd find small piles of them in his closet, under his bed, beneath his kitchen sink, in his backyard. Whenever he'd find them, he'd smash them, not allowing a single one to survive. His entire house was filling with a rotten egg smell so pungent that he had to spend most of his time in the backyard.

One day, while sitting on a lawn chair, hosing off the after-sex stink from his body, somebody came to his door, banging and yelling to be let in. It was the voice of some woman. He didn't bother answering it. Such an issue was better left ignored. But the person at the door did not give up. She went around the side of the house and entered the backyard. She knew he was there. She could smell him.

"You filthy defiler!" she cried, shuffling across the yard toward him.

It was Google's mother. She'd discovered that her daughter had left her old home and had been missing for days. She knew exactly what had happened. It wasn't difficult to track them down.

"You said you had no intention of being with my daughter," she said, standing aggressively with her pinchers out, scuttling side to side like a beach crab. "I knew I shouldn't have trusted you."

Fernando jumped out of his seat and got behind his lawn furniture, using it as a barrier as she closed in on him.

"I'm sorry," he said. "I didn't mean for this to happen."

Google stepped through the broken glass of the sliding door, twitching her antennae at her mother, spraying a pine scent into the air. The mother oozed smells back at her daughter as she spoke to Fernando. It was like she was having two conversations at the same time.

She said, "Maybe you didn't want to marry her, but you still wanted to have sex. Men are all the same, no matter what the species."

She tried to get around the lawn furniture, but Fernando circled to the other side to avoid her pinchers as they snipped the air at him.

"If you don't want us to be together, then just take her and go," Fernando said. "I don't want to be with her. She's ruining my life."

"You're ruining *her* life because you have no self control, you disgusting pig." She snapped her pinchers at him. "I'm going to cut off that thing so that you'll never defile her again."

She seized the lawn chair in her claw and tossed it aside,

leaving Frenando vulnerable.

"Get away from me," he said, stepping back, covering his crotch.

The woman inched forward. "I told you that you'd die if you tried to go after my daughter. Are you ready to die? Was the sex worth it?"

Google tried to get between her mother and her lover, trying to break up the fight. She sprayed dozens of smells at the old lady, but none of them seemed to be getting through. Her mother was plugging her nose so that she wouldn't have to listen.

"Look," Fernando said. "We're matchmates. Every fiber of our beings are driving us to be together. I want to fight it. I really do. But it's hard. We need help. Please, take her away and force her never to come back."

"Do you think I really have that power?" she asked. "Now that you've started mating she's not going to quit until she has her babies. That's how it is with our kind. I can't lock her away until she's too old to mate. She'll find her way back to this house no matter what I do."

"Then I'll move away. I'll disappear. She'll never see me again."

"Do you think I'd actually trust you now? You'd come back to her just as quickly as she'd come back to you. No, there's only one way to separate the two of you. One of you has to die."

Fernando looked at the shovel leaning against the side of his house. It was too far away. He'd never reach it in time. There was only one solution he could come up with.

"Fine," he said. "You can do it."

He pulled his pants on.

The old lady diverted his eyes. "Pull your pants up you disgusting creep."

He stepped toward her. "Cut it off. If that's the only way I can be free of your daughter, then just do it. I want this to end."

Google oozed a tangerine-smelling fluid. She went to

Fernando and pinched at his jeans, trying to pull them up.

"Very well," the old lady said, widening her right claw. "If you're unable to breed with my daughter, I suppose I can let you live."

Google blocked Fernando's key from her mother, protecting it with her shell. She pushed at her mother as the old woman tried to get to her mate's sex organ, squealing and spitting angry foam.

"Out of my way, Goo," the mother said in both languages. "This is what's best. Your vile union must come to an end."

Fernando looked back at his shovel. He wondered if he could get to it in time. He could beat the old woman with it until she ran away, too afraid to ever return, then he could make love to Google for as long as he wanted, for weeks, for years. Nobody would be able to stop him. But then his logical mind came in. If he cut his penis off, then it would all be over. He would no longer be able to have sex with her. He would no longer desire to be with her. She would have no reason to stay with him. There would be no more egg laying, no more chance of being stuck with mutant children, no more decaying stench filling his home. All he had to do was give up his penis.

He pulled himself away from Google and leapt toward the old woman's pinchers. With his eyes closed tight, he waited for the snip and the explosion of pain. But when he heard the pair of claws squeezing together, he did not feel anything. He heard squealing, whining, and the leaking of blood.

The old woman clutched her throat, trying to hold off the blood. Fernando couldn't believe what Google had done. The young tick woman cut her own mother's throat out to prevent her mate from losing his lower appendage.

"You..." the old woman cried, glaring at Fernando, blaming only him for what her daughter had done.

With her last ounce of life, the old woman lunged at Fernando but only made it a few inches before she fell to the ground. Google became like a wild animal. She jumped on top of her mother, opened her mouth of razor sharp dogflesh-digging teeth, then bit into the old lady's throat. She wouldn't stop chewing until her mother's head was separated from her neck. The old lady's antennae continued to wiggle on her severed head as it rolled across the yard.

When Google looked up at Fernando, she breathed heavily. Her exoskeleton pulsed in and out. Her mother's blood dribbled down her chin. She truly was a monster. And though he now found her as frightening as he did disgusting, he couldn't wait to have sex with her again.

Fernando dumped the old woman's body in the tool shed behind his house. He would have chopped it up and tossed it in a dumpster somewhere, but that would have taken too much effort. He wanted to get back to having sex as soon as possible.

There weren't really any laws against killing Ectoparasites. It wasn't something that regularly happened, though. Sometimes an old man would shoot a tick for drinking dog-blood in his backyard. Sometimes they'd get run over on the freeway. Sometimes a group of sexually frustrated teenagers would let off steam by shooting at tick people with hunting rifles. But Ectoparasites killed each other far more often than they were killed by humans. They were insects. Life didn't have much value to them.

If the authorities found out about the dead tick woman in Fernando's tool shed, they'd probably only give him a ticket for causing a health hazard. If Google had killed a human it would have been a different story. They don't take Ectoparasites to jail. When they commit a crime, they were either let free with a warning or killed on the spot, depending on the law that was broken.

The thought of somebody killing Google crossed his mind and he suddenly became paranoid and angry. Anybody could kill her for any reason and there would be no punishment. If he actually stayed with her, married her, had children with her, anybody could kill her at any time. His sister could kill her. Angry mobs who thought their union was unholy could kill her. And he couldn't do anything about it. If he killed somebody while trying to protect her he'd go to jail for life, and she'd probably be executed for being involved. The idea sent chills down his spine. He realized he had to do something about that. He had to speak to the city council, get laws created that protected Ectoparasites, at least for those who were married to humans.

But then Fernando snapped out of it. He remembered that he had no intention of marrying the creature. He didn't even want her in his house any longer. If somebody killed her they would be doing him a great favor.

CHAPTER NINE
IRREPRESSIBLE

It was the first time Fernando tried to give the tick woman oral sex when his sister arrived at his house with the girl she wanted him to meet. He just wanted to see what it was like, licking the puffy tender mounds beneath her lower exoskeleton, pricking his chin against the wiry black hairs that circled the hole. The tick woman wiggled and squirmed as he sucked out her thick fluids, wrapping her lower insect appendages around his waist. She seemed to like it, but tried to get him to stop, trying to pull his body up on top of her so that he could stick his key inside. It was obvious she didn't care for the pleasure if it didn't fertilize her eggs.

"What the hell is going on here?" Bethany's voice echoed through the house as she entered through the broken back door.

"Oh my God…" said another girl's voice. "Do you think he's okay?"

Fernando wanted to pull away, but his matchmate's legs were tightly clutched around his body, like a cicada shell clutching the bark of a tree.

"Fernando? Are you home?" His sister's voice came closer to the bedroom.

"What's that smell?" the other girl asked.

As Fernando tried to crawl up the bug woman's body to get out of her grasp, she wiggled his key into her lock and moaned a buttery odor. Her nipples leaked lubricating fluids against his chest and her lower abdomen throbbed against him. Once inside of her, Fernando didn't care that his sister was in the house. He continued making love to the tick, burying his key into her cavern of goo.

"What the fuck!" Bethany screamed as she pushed open the bedroom door.

Fernando looked over at her. His penis went flaccid. He was shocked back into reality. The two visitors stared at him in horror as he lay there naked atop the writhing bug woman.

The woman behind his sister was the one from the photos. She was all ready for their date—wearing a pretty red dress with matching high heels, her makeup perfectly applied like a girl on a fashion magazine cover, her hair professionally styled as if she'd spent all day at the beauty salon. She was so clean and proper that she clashed against the scum-filled sewer Fernando's house had become.

He wiped the globs of vaginal custard from his nose and said, "What are you doing here?"

He couldn't get out from Google's grasp, so he just pulled the oily blanket over them.

"What do you *think* I'm doing here?" Bethany cried. "You had a date tonight, don't you remember?"

Mary saw a pile of smashed eggs in the corner of the room, the rotten mucus filling her senses, and puked in her hand before she could cover her mouth. She ran out of the room and raced toward the exit, sliding across the floor as she stuck her high heel in a collection of tick shit.

"Mary, wait!" Bethany cried.

But the girl was gone. She ran out of the house and never looked back.

"You're so dead," said his sister.

She wasn't as easily scared off.

"Do you know what you've done?" she asked. "You already ruined that girl's life once. Now it'll never be fixed. You're so selfish."

Fernando was able to pry himself away from the insect woman as she glared at his sister for intruding their home.

"I never wanted to meet her in the first place," Fernando said, as he pulled his pants on beneath the blanket. "That was your crazy idea."

"Crazy? You're calling *me* crazy? You're the one fucking a bug."

She just stood there in the grimy, foul-smelling cesspit, completely unfazed by the environment. Only her brother's bad decisions disturbed her.

"I can't help it," Fernando replied. "Every time I try to kick her out we just end up having sex."

"It's disgusting."

"Yeah, it is. But what am I supposed to do? She's my match-mate. You've been matched. You know what it's like. Would you be able to leave Harry so easily?"

"Harry's a human being, not a tick. I told you not to go meet her. Why didn't you listen to me?"

Fernando looked down. He didn't want to respond.

"I know she wasn't the one who found you. They aren't smart enough to do that. They can't even read addresses."

"You're right. It was stupid. I should've listened to you."

"So what are you going to do now?" she asked. "Make her your wife? Live in this disgusting pit your whole life? Have little baby bugs that carry our family name?"

Google eyeballed his sister, watching her every step. For some reason, she felt threatened by her. Fernando wondered if Ectoparasites were always aggressive toward other females.

"No," he said. "I don't want any of that."

"If word got out about this I'd be a laughing stock," she cried. "You can't let anyone find out about this. I could even lose my job."

"Why would you lose your job?"

She dodged the question. "If you actually married her you'd be dead to me. You know that, right? I will not allow her around my children. I would never want to see you ever again."

"I understand." Fernando stood out of the bed, looking for a shirt. "But what am I supposed to do? It's not easy fighting nature."

Bethany let out a long sigh. "It would have been so perfect… If only you were matched with a real girl… You would have felt this same way for her. You would have had no choice but to get married and have a family. That's what I was hoping for when I got you the appointment with the Matchmaking Bureau. It would have turned you into a normal person."

Fernando shook his head. "You don't understand. I'm not just disgusted with myself because I'm in bed with a tick. I'm disgusted with myself because I can't control my urges. I'd be just as pissed off if I were matched with a human woman."

"But at least then it would be normal."

"I don't care about being normal. I don't want a wife. I don't want to be a slave to my desires. All of it disgusts me."

"Grow up, Little Bro," she said. "You could have used a real woman in your life. Now you've blown it. I have no idea what you're going to do now."

"Can you help?" he asked, stepping toward her. "I can't do it on my own."

Seeing his skin covered in mucus and fishy smells forced her to take a step back. "Well, first we need to get rid of *her*." She pointed at the tick woman who glared at her finger as if she wanted to snip it off. "Then we need to…"

Bethany froze. Something caught her attention on the floor. There was movement.

"What the hell is…" Her voice went soft. Her eyes went cold.

"What?" Fernando asked, trying to see what she was looking at.

Bethany bent down and grabbed it. She lifted it up to waist-level and held it away as it wiggled and squirted tangy smells.

"It's a…" she began.

"A baby?" Fernando cried.

Bethany looked around by her feet. "They're everywhere…"

Fernando saw them, too. They were climbing out of the vents, slithering across the floor. White blubbery tick larvae, their skin so translucent that you could see the fluids pumping inside their bodies. Unlike Google, the baby Bethany held

94

did not yet have a hard exoskeleton. It was soft and pliable. Tiny antennae wiggled on its head. Its insect legs squirmed and kicked. It looked very much like a typical Ectoparasite larva, but instead of pinchers it had human arms, and its bald head looked as if it would one day grow hair.

"Where did they come from?" Fernando asked. His voice was shaking.

"The wall…" Bethany replied.

Fernando realized that Google had successfully hid a batch of eggs from him. She put them through the air vent inside of the wall.

"How could they hatch so quickly?" Fernando asked. "She probably laid those only a few of days ago."

At that moment, Fernando wished he'd paid more attention in class when they taught Ectoparasite anatomy. He knew they could reproduce quickly and in large numbers, but he had no idea just how fast it would happen.

"It's too late…" Bethany said, staring at the squealing wiggly bug in her hand. "You're already a father… You can't leave her now…"

"No, fuck that," Fernando said. "You've got to help me get away from her."

"Don't be an asshole. I know they're bugs, but you've got a responsibility now." She shoved the baby in his face. "You've got to take care of this piece of shit."

The baby squealed in Bethany's grasp and the tick woman lunged out of bed at her. Bethany gasped as the insect mother revealed her fangs, growling, raising her claws as if to cut open her jugular at any second.

"Bethany…" Fernando said, keeping a calm voice as he held Google back. "Slowly… hand the baby over…"

His sister gave him the tick larva, not breaking eye contact with the creature. It was the first time Fernando had ever seen fear in his sister's eyes before. The baby wiggled and squirted a sweet corn smell at her father as he took her in his arms.

"I'm sorry, Little Bro," Bethany said, backing away. "You've made this mess for yourself. Now you've got to live with it."

Fernando looked up at her. "You can't leave me with these things."

From the hallway, she said, "Take care of your disgusting new family…" She turned away. "And keep them the hell away from mine. I don't ever want to see you again."

The tick woman didn't stop foaming until Bethany's smell was out of the house. Fernando looked down at the gurgling bug in his arms. His first thought was to break its neck, throw it in the garbage, burn it in the fireplace. But its body wouldn't let him do any of those things. He held it tightly to his chest to keep it warm. The sound of his heartbeat made the creature feel safe, feel at home.

Fernando couldn't tell if the tick woman was trying to say something to him or if she was emotional at the sight of her child, but her eyes leaked a tear-like fluid. Then she wrapped her claws around the both of them, wiping her eyes against her mate's neck.

CHAPTER TEN
UGLY FRUIT

Sitting in Mr. Olsen's office, wearing his mostly-mucus-free Stressman uniform, covered in the strongest cologne he owned, Fernando stared forward with a blank expression on his face.

"What the hell happened to you?" his boss asked. "You look horrible."

"I'm fine," Fernando said, waiting for his meeting to be over so that he could get back to his cesspool of a home life.

Mr. Olsen let out a sigh and leaned back in his chair. "I've been following the story about you in the news. Is it true? You really got married to that tick you were matched with?"

"I didn't have a choice," Fernando said. "It was the only way to stop the religious fanatics from cutting my wife's head off and burning my children at the stake."

"Yeah, I heard they passed those new laws for you. I'm glad things are going to be okay now."

"It's not going to be okay," he said. "In all honesty, I'd be better off if they did kill her and the kids. They're miserable, disgusting things."

"Yeah, well they're *your* miserable, disgusting things."

"I know."

Fernando looked out the window at Old Gloomy as Stressmen taunted him, calling him names and breaking dog toys in front of him. He empathized with the old dog. He knew exactly what it was like to suffer through a life of misery.

"Well, now that you have so many mouths to feed I guess you're in need of a paycheck."

"Not really. They're parasites. They drink their meals out of the ground."

Mr. Olsen looked away. Fernando could tell he was disgusted by the thought of a dozen tick babies feeding on dog blood inside of a human home.

"But you still want your old job back, don't you?"

"Of course I do. I'm a Stressman, like my father and my grandfather before me. It was what I was born to be."

"Good," Mr. Olsen said, nodding his head. "Because I'd like to give you another chance. I think your time off did you some good. In fact, I don't think I've ever seen a Stressman more depressed."

Fernando shrugged.

"I mean it, you look downright *miserable*."

Fernando shrugged again.

"I'd like you to come in bright and early on Monday," Olsen said. "Don't worry about bringing any new ideas. Just come in with an old standby sadness treatment and we'll see how it goes."

"Sure," Fernando said.

He stood up and put out his hand to shake, but the boss waved it away.

"And try to find a better way to cover up that stink on you," Olsen said. "Your cologne isn't quite strong enough."

Fernando lowered his hand. "I'll see what I can do."

On the way out, Fernando passed Old Gloomy's face and looked up into the dog's massive eyes. With just one glance, Gloomy saw the cold, depressing emotions oozing from the man with the parasitic bride. The sadness was contagious. All it took was one look upon the Stressman for the old dog to burst into tears.

"Yes," said Mr. Olsen, nodding his head at the sight. "I think you'll do just fine, Mr. Mendez. If your attitude keeps up, maybe you'll even take over my job someday."

Fernando just nodded and walked on. It used to excite

him, make him feel accomplished, even heroic, whenever he made Old Gloomy cry. But as the dog's tears rained into the canals below, he felt nothing.

When Fernando got home, he squeezed past the dozens of wiggling larvae infesting his home, half of them gorging on blood on the living room floor, poking up in the air like fat white balloons of flesh.

"Goo?" Fernando called out.

He couldn't wait to be with her again.

"Where are you?"

She was right where he expected she would be—waiting for him in the bedroom. He hated the sight of her. He hated the look of her sitting on his bed, rubbing her lower abdomen with those twitchy spider-like appendages. But he hated himself even more as got on top of her and put his key into her sludgy custard-filled lock.

As they mated, he could feel sticky round orbs rubbing against the tip of his penis deep inside of her. Fernando didn't notice it before, but this time he realized that those globby balls of mucus deep in her gooey hole were actually her eggs. He was fucking her egg sack. And as he shoved himself deeper inside, the idea of ejaculating onto all of those eggs, fertilizing them, turning them into mutant babies, only made him more erect. It took him just another minute before he exploded, filling her arachnid egg sack with his human seed.

As he finished and rolled off of her onto the greasy sheets, she got up and left the bed. She didn't care about cuddling. She didn't care about holding him in her thorny arms. She just wanted to tend to her children and lay another batch of eggs.

Fernando just stayed there. He had no reason to get up. He just looked up at the ceiling, thinking about all the reasons he loathed himself, wondering if there was any way he'd ever get over his need for the creature's body. Eventually, his wife would come back to him and they'd do it again. He wouldn't resist. He would gladly give himself over to the urge, every single time. He wasn't strong enough to do otherwise.

Although Ectoparasites didn't really understand the concept of love or happiness, Google was very satisfied having Fernando as her mate. Now that he no longer smashed her eggs, Fernando provided her with many healthy children in a safe environment. Her offspring would prove to have a high survival rate, which was all that Ectoparasite mothers could ever want. She would likely be the first tick woman in history to birth children in the hundreds.

But Fernando didn't really care about that. He would never stop loathing himself or his grotesque family. He would give up on happiness and put all of his attention into being the best Stressman he could be. His wife would fill him with misery and he'd take that misery with him to work every day. And because of his despair, he would keep the town of Gloomsville safe for the rest of his life. He would prove to be the greatest Stressman who ever lived.

And although Fernando would never admit it, deep down he knew that everything about his relationship with the tick woman was just right. They truly were a perfect match.

BONUS SECTION

This is the part of the book where we would have published an afterword by the author but he insisted on drawing a comic strip instead for reasons we don't quite understand.

Thank you for reading my new book, *The Tick People*. Wasn't it saucy?

It's me CM3!

just finished reading it

the tick people

the tick

WHAT THE FUCK KIND OF PERVERTED BULLSHIT WAS THAT!!

the tick people

You didn't like it?

Hell no! Erotica is supposed to be sexy. Those were the least sexy sex scenes I've ever read!

I think it's sexy.

THE END

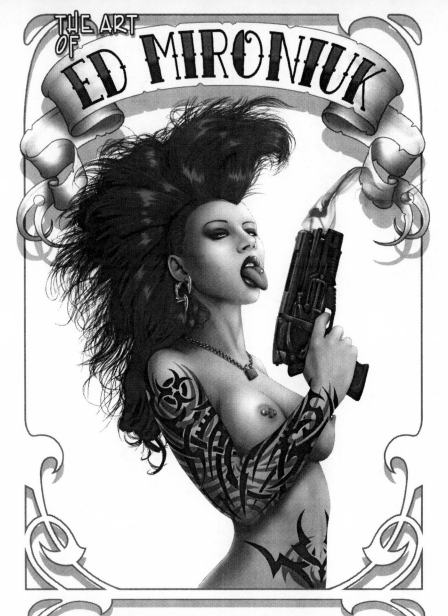

ABOUT THE AUTHOR

Carlton Mellick III is one of the leading authors of the bizarro fiction subgenre. Since 2001, his books have drawn an international cult following, despite the fact that they have been shunned by most libraries and chain bookstores.

He won the Wonderland Book Award for his novel, *Warrior Wolf Women of the Wasteland*, in 2009. His short fiction has appeared in *Vice Magazine, The Year's Best Fantasy and Horror #16, The Magazine of Bizarro Fiction*, and *Zombies: Encounters with the Hungry Dead*, among others. He is also a graduate of Clarion West, where he studied under the likes of Chuck Palahniuk, Connie Willis, and Cory Doctorow.

He lives in Portland, OR, the bizarro fiction mecca.

Visit him online at **www.carltonmellick.com**

BIZARRO BOOKS

CATALOG   SPRING 2013

**ERASERHEAD
PRESS**

Your major resource for the bizarro fiction genre:

WWW.BIZARROCENTRAL.COM

Introduce yourselves to the bizarro fiction genre and all of its authors with the Bizarro Starter Kit series. Each volume features short novels and short stories by ten of the leading bizarro authors, designed to give you a perfect sampling of the genre for only $10.

BB-0X1
"The Bizarro Starter Kit"
(Orange)
Featuring D. Harlan Wilson, Carlton Mellick III, Jeremy Robert Johnson, Kevin L Donihe, Gina Ranalli, Andre Duza, Vincent W. Sakowski, Steve Beard, John Edward Lawson, and Bruce Taylor.
236 pages $10

BB-0X2
"The Bizarro Starter Kit"
(Blue)
Featuring Ray Fracalossy, Jeremy C. Shipp, Jordan Krall, Mykle Hansen, Andersen Prunty, Eckhard Gerdes, Bradley Sands, Steve Aylett, Christian TeBordo, and Tony Rauch. **244 pages $10**

BB-0X2
"The Bizarro Starter Kit"
(Purple)
Featuring Russell Edson, Athena Villaverde, David Agranoff, Matthew Revert, Andrew Goldfarb, Jeff Burk, Garrett Cook, Kris Saknussemm, Cody Goodfellow, and Cameron Pierce **264 pages $10**

BB-001"The Kafka Effekt" D. Harlan Wilson — A collection of forty-four irreal short stories loosely written in the vein of Franz Kafka, with more than a pinch of William S. Burroughs sprinkled on top. **211 pages $14**

BB-002 "Satan Burger" Carlton Mellick III — The cult novel that put Carlton Mellick III on the map ... Six punks get jobs at a fast food restaurant owned by the devil in a city violently overpopulated by surreal alien cultures. **236 pages $14**

BB-003 "Some Things Are Better Left Unplugged" Vincent Sakwoski — Join The Man and his Nemesis, the obese tabby, for a nightmare roller coaster ride into this postmodern fantasy. **152 pages $10**

BB-005 "Razor Wire Pubic Hair" Carlton Mellick III — A genderless humandildo is purchased by a razor dominatrix and brought into her nightmarish world of bizarre sex and mutilation. **176 pages $11**

BB-007 "The Baby Jesus Butt Plug" Carlton Mellick III — Using clones of the Baby Jesus for anal sex will be the hip sex fetish of the future. **92 pages $10**

BB-010 "The Menstruating Mall" Carlton Mellick III — "The Breakfast Club meets Chopping Mall as directed by David Lynch." - Brian Keene **212 pages $12**

BB-011 "Angel Dust Apocalypse" Jeremy Robert Johnson — Meth-heads, man-made monsters, and murderous Neo-Nazis. "Seriously amazing short stories..." - Chuck Palahniuk, author of Fight Club **184 pages $11**

BB-015 "Foop!" Chris Genoa — Strange happenings are going on at Dactyl, Inc, the world's first and only time travel tourism company.
"A surreal pie in the face!" - Christopher Moore **300 pages $14**

BB-032 **"Extinction Journals" Jeremy Robert Johnson** — An uncanny voyage across a newly nuclear America where one man must confront the problems associated with loneliness, insane dieties, radiation, love, and an ever-evolving cockroach suit with a mind of its own. **104 pages $10**

BB-037 **"The Haunted Vagina" Carlton Mellick III** — It's difficult to love a woman whose vagina is a gateway to the world of the dead. **132 pages $10**

BB-043 **"War Slut" Carlton Mellick III** — Part "1984," part "Waiting for Godot," and part action horror video game adaptation of John Carpenter's "The Thing." **116 pages $10**

BB-047 **"Sausagey Santa" Carlton Mellick III** — A bizarro Christmas tale featuring Santa as a piratey mutant with a body made of sausages. 124 pages $10

BB-048 **"Misadventures in a Thumbnail Universe" Vincent Sakowski** — Dive deep into the surreal and satirical realms of neo-classical Blender Fiction, filled with television shoes and flesh-filled skies. **120 pages $10**

BB-053 **"Ballad of a Slow Poisoner" Andrew Goldfarb** — Millford Mutterwurst sat down on a Tuesday to take his afternoon tea, and made the unpleasant discovery that his elbows were becoming flatter. **128 pages $10**

BB-055 **"Help! A Bear is Eating Me" Mykle Hansen** — The bizarro, heartwarming, magical tale of poor planning, hubris and severe blood loss... **150 pages $11**

BB-056 **"Piecemeal June" Jordan Krall** — A man falls in love with a living sex doll, but with love comes danger when her creator comes after her with crab-squid assassins. **90 pages $9**

BB-058 **"The Overwhelming Urge" Andersen Prunty** — A collection of bizarro tales by Andersen Prunty. **150 pages $11**

BB-059 **"Adolf in Wonderland" Carlton Mellick III** — A dreamlike adventure that takes a young descendant of Adolf Hitler's design and sends him down the rabbit hole into a world of imperfection and disorder. **180 pages $11**

BB-061 **"Ultra Fuckers" Carlton Mellick III** — Absurdist suburban horror about a couple who enter an upper middle class gated community but can't find their way out. **108 pages $9**

BB-062 **"House of Houses" Kevin L. Donihe** — An odd man wants to marry his house. Unfortunately, all of the houses in the world collapse at the same time in the Great House Holocaust. Now he must travel to House Heaven to find his departed fiancee. **172 pages $11**

BB-064 **"Squid Pulp Blues" Jordan Krall** — In these three bizarro-noir novellas, the reader is thrown into a world of murderers, drugs made from squid parts, deformed gun-toting veterans, and a mischievous apocalyptic donkey. **204 pages $12**

BB-065 **"Jack and Mr. Grin" Andersen Prunty** — "When Mr. Grin calls you can hear a smile in his voice. Not a warm and friendly smile, but the kind that seizes your spine in fear. You don't need to pay your phone bill to hear it. That smile is in every line of Prunty's prose." - Tom Bradley. **208 pages $12**

BB-066 **"Cybernetrix" Carlton Mellick III** — What would you do if your normal everyday world was slowly mutating into the video game world from Tron? **212 pages $12**

BB-072 **"Zerostrata" Andersen Prunty** — Hansel Nothing lives in a tree house, suffers from memory loss, has a very eccentric family, and falls in love with a woman who runs naked through the woods every night. **144 pages $11**

BB-073 **"The Egg Man" Carlton Mellick III** — It is a world where humans reproduce like insects. Children are the property of corporations, and having an enormous ten-foot brain implanted into your skull is a grotesque sexual fetish. Mellick's industrial urban dystopia is one of his darkest and grittiest to date. **184 pages $11**

BB-074 **"Shark Hunting in Paradise Garden" Cameron Pierce** — A group of strange humanoid religious fanatics travel back in time to the Garden of Eden to discover it is invested with hundreds of giant flying maneating sharks. **150 pages $10**

BB-075 **"Apeshit" Carlton Mellick III** - Friday the 13th meets Visitor Q. Six hipster teens go to a cabin in the woods inhabited by a deformed killer. An incredibly fucked-up parody of B-horror movies with a bizarro slant. **192 pages $12**

BB-076 **"Fuckers of Everything on the Crazy Shitting Planet of the Vomit At smosphere" Mykle Hansen** - Three bizarro satires. Monster Cocks, Journey to the Center of Agnes Cuddlebottom, and Crazy Shitting Planet. **228 pages $12**

BB-077 **"The Kissing Bug" Daniel Scott Buck** — In the tradition of Roald Dahl, Tim Burton, and Edward Gorey, comes this bizarro anti-war children's story about a bohemian conenose kissing bug who falls in love with a human woman. **116 pages $10**

BB-078 **"MachoPoni" Lotus Rose** — It's My Little Pony... *Bizarro* style! A long time ago Poniworld was split in two. On one side of the Jagged Line is the Pastel Kingdom, a magical land of music, parties, and positivity. On the other side of the Jagged Line is Dark Kingdom inhabited by an army of undead ponies. **148 pages $11**

BB-079 **"The Faggiest Vampire" Carlton Mellick III** — A Roald Dahl-esque children's story about two faggy vampires who partake in a mustache competition to find out which one is truly the faggiest. **104 pages $10**

BB-080 **"Sky Tongues" Gina Ranalli** — The autobiography of Sky Tongues, the biracial hermaphrodite actress with tongues for fingers. Follow her strange life story as she rises from freak to fame. **204 pages $12**

BB-081 **"Washer Mouth" Kevin L. Donihe** - A washing machine becomes human and pursues his dream of meeting his favorite soap opera star. **244 pages $11**

BB-082 **"Shatnerquake" Jeff Burk** - All of the characters ever played by William Shatner are suddenly sucked into our world. Their mission: hunt down and destroy the real William Shatner. **100 pages $10**

BB-083 **"The Cannibals of Candyland" Carlton Mellick III** - There exists a race of cannibals that are made of candy. They live in an underground world made out of candy. One man has dedicated his life to killing them all. **170 pages $11**

BB-084 **"Slub Glub in the Weird World of the Weeping Willows" Andrew Goldfarb** - The charming tale of a blue glob named Slub Glub who helps the weeping willows whose tears are flooding the earth. There are also hyenas, ghosts, and a voodoo priest **100 pages $10**

BB-085 **"Super Fetus" Adam Pepper** - Try to abort this fetus and he'll kick your ass! **104 pages $10**

BB-086 **"Fistful of Feet" Jordan Krall** - A bizarre tribute to spaghetti westerns, featuring Cthulhu-worshipping Indians, a woman with four feet, a crazed gunman who is obsessed with sucking on candy, Syphilis-ridden mutants, sexually transmitted tattoos, and a house devoted to the freakiest fetishes. **228 pages $12**

BB-087 **"Ass Goblins of Auschwitz" Cameron Pierce** - It's Monty Python meets Nazi exploitation in a surreal nightmare as can only be imagined by Bizarro author Cameron Pierce. **104 pages $10**

BB-088 **"Silent Weapons for Quiet Wars" Cody Goodfellow** - "This is high-end psychological surrealist horror meets bottom-feeding low-life crime in a techno-thrilling science fiction world full of Lovecraft and magic..." -John Skipp **212 pages $12**

BB-089 "Warrior Wolf Women of the Wasteland" Carlton Mellick III
— Road Warrior Werewolves versus McDonaldland Mutants...post-apocalyptic fiction has never been quite like this. 316 pages $13

BB-091 "Super Giant Monster Time" Jeff Burk — A tribute to choose your own adventures and Godzilla movies. Will you escape the giant monsters that are rampaging the fuck out of your city and shit? Or will you join the mob of alien-controlled punk rockers causing chaos in the streets? What happens next depends on you. 188 pages $12

BB-092 "Perfect Union" Cody Goodfellow — "Cronenberg's THE FLY on a grand scale: human/insect gene-spliced body horror, where the human hive politics are as shocking as the gore." -John Skipp. 272 pages $13

BB-093 "Sunset with a Beard" Carlton Mellick III — 14 stories of surreal science fiction. 200 pages $12

BB-094 "My Fake War" Andersen Prunty — The absurd tale of an unlikely soldier forced to fight a war that, quite possibly, does not exist. It's Rambo meets Waiting for Godot in this subversive satire of American values and the scope of the human imagination. 128 pages $11

BB-095 "Lost in Cat Brain Land" Cameron Pierce — Sad stories from a sur-real world. A fascist mustache, the ghost of Franz Kafka, a desert inside a dead cat. Primordial entities mourn the death of their child. The desperate serve tea to mysterious creatures. A hopeless romantic falls in love with a pterodactyl. And much more. 152 pages $11

BB-096 "The Kobold Wizard's Dildo of Enlightenment +2" Carlton Mellick III — A Dungeons and Dragons parody about a group of people who learn they are only made up characters in an AD&D campaign and must find a way to resist their nerdy teenaged players and retarded dungeon master in order to survive. 232 pages $12

BB-098 "A Hundred Horrible Sorrows of Ogner Stump" Andrew Goldfarb — Goldfarb's acclaimed comic series. A magical and weird journey into the horrors of everyday life. 164 pages $11

BB-099 **"Pickled Apocalypse of Pancake Island" Cameron Pierce**—A demented fairy tale about a pickle, a pancake, and the apocalypse. **102 pages $8**

BB-100 **"Slag Attack" Andersen Prunty**— Slag Attack features four visceral, noir stories about the living, crawling apocalypse. A slag is what survivors are calling the slug-like maggots raining from the sky, burrowing inside people, and hollowing out their flesh and their sanity. **148 pages $11**

BB-101 **"Slaughterhouse High" Robert Devereaux**—A place where schools are built with secret passageways, rebellious teens get zippers installed in their mouths and genitals, and once a year, on that special night, one couple is slaughtered and the bits of their bodies are kept as souvenirs. **304 pages $13**

BB-102 **"The Emerald Burrito of Oz" John Skipp & Marc Levinthal** —OZ IS REAL! Magic is real! The gate is really in Kansas! And America is finally allowing Earth tourists to visit this weird-ass, mysterious land. But when Gene of Los Angeles heads off for summer vacation in the Emerald City, little does he know that a war is brewing...a war that could destroy both worlds. **280 pages $13**

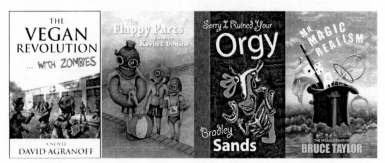

BB-103 **"The Vegan Revolution... with Zombies" David Agranoff** — When there's no more meat in hell, the vegans will walk the earth. **160 pages $11**

BB-104 **"The Flappy Parts" Kevin L Donihe**—Poems about bunnies, LSD, and police abuse. You know, things that matter. 132 **pages $11**

BB-105 **"Sorry I Ruined Your Orgy" Bradley Sands**—Bizarro humorist Bradley Sands returns with one of the strangest, most hilarious collections of the year. **130 pages $11**

BB-106 **"Mr. Magic Realism" Bruce Taylor**—Like Golden Age science fiction comics written by Freud, *Mr. Magic Realism* is a strange, insightful adventure that spans the furthest reaches of the galaxy, exploring the hidden caverns in the hearts and minds of men, women, aliens, and biomechanical cats. **152 pages $11**

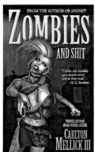   

BB-107 **"Zombies and Shit" Carlton Mellick III**—"Battle Royale" meets "Return of the Living Dead." Mellick's bizarro tribute to the zombie genre. **308 pages $13**

BB-108 **"The Cannibal's Guide to Ethical Living" Mykle Hansen**— Over a five star French meal of fine wine, organic vegetables and human flesh, a lunatic delivers a witty, chilling, disturbingly sane argument in favor of eating the rich.. **184 pages $11**

BB-109 **"Starfish Girl" Athena Villaverde**—In a post-apocalyptic underwater dome society, a girl with a starfish growing from her head and an assassin with sea anenome hair are on the run from a gang of mutant fish men. **160 pages $11**

BB-110 **"Lick Your Neighbor" Chris Genoa**—Mutant ninjas, a talking whale, kung fu masters, maniacal pilgrims, and an alcoholic clown populate Chris Genoa's surreal, darkly comical and unnerving reimagining of the first Thanksgiving. **303 pages $13**

BB-111 **"Night of the Assholes" Kevin L. Donihe**—A plague of assholes is infecting the countryside. Normal everyday people are transforming into jerks, snobs, dicks, and douchebags. And they all have only one purpose: to make your life a living hell.. **192 pages $11**

BB-112 **"Jimmy Plush, Teddy Bear Detective" Garrett Cook**—Hard-boiled cases of a private detective trapped within a teddy bear body. **180 pages $11**

BB-113 **"The Deadheart Shelters" Forrest Armstrong**—The hip hop lovechild of William Burroughs and Dali... **144 pages $11**

BB-114 **"Eyeballs Growing All Over Me... Again" Tony Raugh**— Absurd, surreal, playful, dream-like, whimsical, and a lot of fun to read. **144 pages $11**

BB-115 **"Whargoul" Dave Brockie** — From the killing grounds of Stalingrad to the death camps of the holocaust. From torture chambers in Iraq to race riots in the United States, the Whargoul was there, killing and raping. **244 pages $12**

BB-116 **"By the Time We Leave Here, We'll Be Friends" J. David Osborne** — A David Lynchian nightmare set in a Russian gulag, where its prisoners, guards, traitors, soldiers, lovers, and demons fight for survival and their own rapidly deteriorating humanity. **168 pages $11**

BB-117 **"Christmas on Crack" edited by Carlton Mellick III** — Perverted Christmas Tales for the whole family! . . . as long as every member of your family is over the age of 18. **168 pages $11**

BB-118 **"Crab Town" Carlton Mellick III** — Radiation fetishists, balloon people, mutant crabs, sail-bike road warriors, and a love affair between a woman and an H-Bomb. This is one mean asshole of a city. Welcome to Crab Town. **100 pages $8**

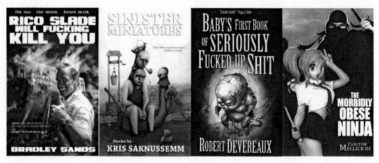

BB-119 **"Rico Slade Will Fucking Kill You" Bradley Sands** — Rico Slade is an action hero. Rico Slade can rip out a throat with his bare hands. Rico Slade's favorite food is the honey-roasted peanut. Rico Slade will fucking kill everyone. A novel. **122 pages $8**

BB-120 **"Sinister Miniatures" Kris Saknussemm** — The definitive collection of short fiction by Kris Saknussemm, confirming that he is one of the best, most daring writers of the weird to emerge in the twenty-first century. **180 pages $11**

BB-121 **"Baby's First Book of Seriously Fucked up Shit" Robert Devereaux** — Ten stories of the strange, the gross, and the just plain fucked up from one of the most original voices in horror. **176 pages $11**

BB-122 **"The Morbidly Obese Ninja" Carlton Mellick III** — These days, if you want to run a successful company . . . you're going to need a lot of ninjas. **92 pages $8**

BB-123 **"Abortion Arcade" Cameron Pierce** — An intoxicating blend of body horror and midnight movie madness, reminiscent of early David Lynch and the splatterpunks at their most sublime. **172 pages $11**

BB-124 **"Black Hole Blues" Patrick Wensink** — A hilarious double helix of country music and physics. **196 pages $11**

BB-125 **"Barbarian Beast Bitches of the Badlands" Carlton Mellick III** — Three prequels and sequels to *Warrior Wolf Women of the Wasteland*. **284 pages $13**

BB-126 **"The Traveling Dildo Salesman" Kevin L. Donihe** — A nightmare comedy about destiny, faith, and sex toys. Also featuring Donihe's most lurid and infamous short stories: *Milky Agitation, Two-Way Santa, The Helen Mower, Living Room Zombies,* and *Revenge of the Living Masturbation Rag.* **108 pages $8**

BB-127 **"Metamorphosis Blues" Bruce Taylor** — Enter a land of love beasts, intergalactic cowboys, and rock 'n roll. A land where Sears Catalogs are doorways to insanity and men keep mysterious black boxes. Welcome to the monstrous mind of Mr. Magic Realism. **136 pages $11**

BB-128 **"The Driver's Guide to Hitting Pedestrians" Andersen Prunty** — A pocket guide to the twenty-three most painful things in life, written by the most well-adjusted man in the universe. **108 pages $8**

BB-129 **"Island of the Super People" Kevin Shamel** — Four students and their anthropology professor journey to a remote island to study its indigenous population. But this is no ordinary native culture. They're super heroes and villains with flesh costumes and out-landish abilities like self-detonation, musical eyelashes, and microwave hands. **194 pages $11**

BB-130 **"Fantastic Orgy" Carlton Mellick III** — Shark Sex, mutant cats, and strange sexually transmitted diseases. Featuring the stories: *Candy-coated, Ear Cat, Fantastic Orgy, City Hobgoblins,* and *Porno in August.* **136 pages $9**

BB-131 "Cripple Wolf" Jeff Burk — Part man. Part wolf. 100% crippled. Also including *Punk Rock Nursing Home, Adrift with Space Badgers, Cook for Your Life, Just Another Day in the Park, Frosty and the Full Monty,* and *House of Cats.* **152 pages $10**

BB-132 "I Knocked Up Satan's Daughter" Carlton Mellick III — An adorable, violent, fantastical love story. A romantic comedy for the bizarro fiction reader. **152 pages $10**

BB-133 "A Town Called Suckhole" David W. Barbee — Far into the future, in the nuclear bowels of post-apocalyptic Dixie, there is a town. A town of derelict mobile homes, ancient junk, and mutant wildlife. A town of slack jawed rednecks who bask in the splendors of moonshine and mud boggin'. A town dedicated to the bloody and demented legacy of the Old South. A town called Suckhole. **144 pages $10**

BB-134 "Cthulhu Comes to the Vampire Kingdom" Cameron Pierce — What you'd get if H. P. Lovecraft wrote a Tim Burton animated film. **148 pages $11**

BB-135 "I am Genghis Cum" Violet LeVoit — From the savage Arctic tundra to post-partum mutations to your missing daughter's unmarked grave, join visionary madwoman Violet LeVoit in this non-stop eight-story onslaught of full-tilt Bizarro punk lit thrills. **124 pages $9**

BB-136 "Haunt" Laura Lee Bahr — A tripping-balls Los Angeles noir, where a mysterious dame drags you through a time-warping Bizarro hall of mirrors. **316 pages $13**

BB-137 "Amazing Stories of the Flying Spaghetti Monster" edited by Cameron Pierce — Like an all-spaghetti evening of Adult Swim, the Flying Spaghetti Monster will show you the many realms of His Noodly Appendage. Learn of those who worship him and the lives he touches in distant, mysterious ways. **228 pages $12**

BB-138 "Wave of Mutilation" Douglas Lain — A dream-pop exploration of modern architecture and the American identity, *Wave of Mutilation* is a Zen finger trap for the 21st century. **100 pages $8**

BB-139 "Hooray for Death!" Mykle Hansen — Famous Author Mykle Hansen draws unconventional humor from deaths tiny and large, and invites you to laugh while you can. **128 pages $10**

BB-140 "Hypno-hog's Moonshine Monster Jamboree" Andrew Goldfarb — Hicks, Hogs, Horror! Goldfarb is back with another strange illustrated tale of backwoods weirdness. **120 pages $9**

BB-141 "Broken Piano For President" Patrick Wensink — A comic masterpiece about the fast food industry, booze, and the necessity to choose happiness over work and security. **372 pages $15**

BB-142 "Please Do Not Shoot Me in the Face" Bradley Sands — A novel in three parts, *Please Do Not Shoot Me in the Face: A Novel*, is the story of one boy detective, the worst ninja in the world, and the great American fast food wars. It is a novel of loss, destruction, and--incredibly--genuine hope. **224 pages $12**

BB-143 "Santa Steps Out" Robert Devereaux — Sex, Death, and Santa Claus ... The ultimate erotic Christmas story is back. **294 pages $13**

BB-144 "Santa Conquers the Homophobes" Robert Devereaux — "I wish I could hope to ever attain one-thousandth the perversity of Robert Devereaux's toenail clippings." - Poppy Z. Brite **316 pages $13**

BB-145 "We Live Inside You" Jeremy Robert Johnson — "Jeremy Robert Johnson is dancing to a way different drummer. He loves language, he loves the edge, and he loves us people. These stories have range and style and wit. This is entertainment... and literature."- Jack Ketchum **188 pages $11**

BB-146 "Clockwork Girl" Athena Villaverde — Urban fairy tales for the weird girl in all of us. Like a combination of Francesca Lia Block, Charles de Lint, Kathe Koja, Tim Burton, and Hayao Miyazaki, her stories are cute, kinky, edgy, magical, provocative, and strange, full of poetic imagery and vicious sexuality. **160 pages $10**

BB-147 **"Armadillo Fists" Carlton Mellick III** — A weird-as-hell gangster story set in a world where people drive giant mechanical dinosaurs instead of cars. **168 pages $11**

BB-148 **"Gargoyle Girls of Spider Island" Cameron Pierce** — Four college seniors venture out into open waters for the tropical party weekend of a lifetime. Instead of a teenage sex fantasy, they find themselves in a nightmare of pirates, sharks, and sex-crazed monsters. **100 pages $8**

BB-149 **"The Handsome Squirm" by Carlton Mellick III** — Like Franz Kafka's *The Trial* meets an erotic body horror version of *The Blob.* **158 pages $11**

BB-150 **"Tentacle Death Trip" Jordan Krall** — It's *Death Race 2000* meets H. P. Lovecraft in bizarro author Jordan Krall's best and most suspenseful work to date. **224 pages $12**

BB-151 **"The Obese" Nick Antosca** — Like Alfred Hitchcock's *The Birds*... but with obese people. **108 pages $10**

BB-152 **"All-Monster Action!" Cody Goodfellow** — The world gave him a blank check and a demand: Create giant monsters to fight our wars. But Dr. Otaku was not satisfied with mere chaos and mass destruction.... **216 pages $12**

BB-153 **"Ugly Heaven" Carlton Mellick III** — Heaven is no longer a paradise. It was once a blissful utopia full of wonders far beyond human comprehension. But the afterlife is now in ruins. It has become an ugly, lonely wasteland populated by strange monstrous beasts, masturbating angels, and sad man-like beings wallowing in the remains of the once-great Kingdom of God. **106 pages $8**

BB-154 **"Space Walrus" Kevin L. Donihe** — Walter is supposed to go where no walrus has ever gone before, but all this astronaut walrus really wants is to take it easy on the intense training, escape the chimpanzee bullies, and win the love of his human trainer Dr. Stephanie. **160 pages $11**

BB-155 **"Unicorn Battle Squad" Kirsten Alene** — Mutant unicorns. A palace with a thousand human legs. The most powerful army on the planet. **192 pages $11**

BB-156 **"Kill Ball" Carlton Mellick III** — In a city where all humans live inside of plastic bubbles, exotic dancers are being murdered in the rubbery streets by a mysterious stalker known only as Kill Ball. **134 pages $10**

BB-157 **"Die You Doughnut Bastards" Cameron Pierce** — The bacon storm is rolling in. We hear the grease and sugar beat against the roof and windows. The doughnut people are attacking. We press close together, forgetting for a moment that we hate each other. **196 pages $11**

BB-158 **"Tumor Fruit" Carlton Mellick III** — Eight desperate castaways find themselves stranded on a mysterious deserted island. They are surrounded by poisonous blue plants and an ocean made of acid. Ravenous creatures lurk in the toxic jungle. The ghostly sound of crying babies can be heard on the wind. **310 pages $13**

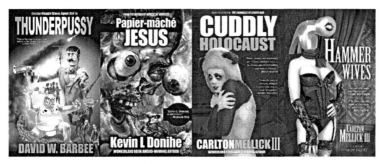

BB-159 **"Thunderpussy" David W. Barbee** — When it comes to high-tech global espionage, only one man has the balls to save humanity from the world's most powerful bastards. He's Declan Magpie Bruce, Agent 00X. **136 pages $11**

BB-160 **"Papier Mâché Jesus" Kevin L. Donihe** — Donihe's surreal wit and beautiful mind-bending imagination is on full display with stories such as All Children Go to Hell, Happiness is a Warm Gun, and Swimming in Endless Night. **154 pages $11**

BB-161 **"Cuddly Holocaust" Carlton Mellick III** — The war between humans and toys has come to an end. The toys won. **172 pages $11**

BB-162 **"Hammer Wives" Carlton Mellick III** — Fish-eyed mutants, oceans of insects, and flesh-eating women with hammers for heads. Hammer Wives collects six of his most popular novelettes and short stories. **152 pages $10**

CPSIA information can be obtained at www.ICGtesting.com
Printed in the USA
BVOW01s1922030414

349685BV00001B/5/P